"There's only one way to find out if we're soul mates, Lydia.

"And that," Joe continued, "is to get a bit closer."

Lydia went to stand up, but stilled as he spoke again.

"You opened your heart just a little to let me kiss you, because you couldn't help it. Then you closed all channels of communication like a clam."

She licked her lips. "Perhaps it's the only way I feel I can handle you, Joe."

She saw his gaze narrow. "Then may I take another approach?" Joe said consideringly. "Having once kissed you without your permission—"

"Joe Jordan, kiss me before I change my mind!" she advised.

Legally wed,
but he's never said…
"I love you."

They're…

The series where marriages are made in haste…
and love comes later….

Look out for our next great
Wedlocked! title.

Coming soon!

Lindsay Armstrong

THE UNEXPECTED HUSBAND

TORONTO • NEW YORK • LONDON
AMSTERDAM • PARIS • SYDNEY • HAMBURG
STOCKHOLM • ATHENS • TOKYO • MILAN • MADRID
PRAGUE • WARSAW • BUDAPEST • AUCKLAND

ISBN 0-373-12156-3

THE UNEXPECTED HUSBAND

First North American Publication 2001.

This edition published by arrangement with Harlequin Books S.A.

® and TM are trademarks of the publisher. Trademarks indicated with
® are registered in the United States Patent and Trademark Office, the
Canadian Trade Marks Office and in other countries.

Visit us at www.eHarlequin.com

Printed in U.S.A.

CHAPTER ONE

'OF COURSE I don't want to go to bed with you!' Lydia Kelso said.

Joe Jordan stared at the woman who had just rejected his offer with such stinging contempt, and he registered mental surprise tinged with amusement. Surprise because Lydia Kelso was as different from her sister as chalk from cheese...

She had an unruly mane of sun-streaked dark fair hair that looked as if she didn't bother to torture it into any kind of style. Her skin was smooth and her eyes a deep velvety blue. Whilst she didn't have immediately turn-your-head kind of looks, that lovely skin, the delicately cut yet severe pair of lips, as well as her stunning eyes, redeemed her to a rather unusual attractiveness. She wore no make-up at all.

Her neck was long and elegant—so was the rest of her: tall and almost boyishly rangy beneath a pinstriped navy trouser suit she wore with black leather loafers. Her shoulders were straight and her hands were narrow yet capable-looking, with short, unpainted nails, and she wore a man's signet ring on the little finger of her left hand and a man's watch.

Whereas her sister Daisy was drop-dead gorgeous, with dark hair, true violet eyes and a sensational figure...

He shrugged, raised an ironic eyebrow at Lydia Kelso, and murmured, 'I asked because that was the proposition your sister put to *me* when we first met. I thought it might run in the family.'

'You should never generalise about people, even when they come from the same family, Mr Jordan,' she said coldly.

'Does that mean you don't approve of your own sister?' he asked wryly.

Lydia took a breath and subsided somewhat. Then she moved her hands and decided to be honest. 'I don't approve of you,' she said flatly.

'We've only just met,' he pointed out, with open amusement in his eyes now.

'Your reputation precedes you, however, so—'

'All right.' He sat up straighter and reached for his pen. 'Tell me exactly what you know about me, Lydia Kelso. We may then be able to sort the wheat from the chaff.'

Lydia looked around Joe Jordan's colourful studio and reflected that she could have been outmanoeuvred. At the same time she took in the posters on the wall, the books and magazines overflowing from a whole wall of honey pine bookshelves, the polished timber floor with a slightly ruckled rug in jewel-bright ruby swirls on a yellow background. There were two computers on the table behind him, an easel, a skylight above, and a particularly healthy Kentia palm flourishing in a wicker basket in one corner.

Then she looked back at him across the wide expanse of his untidy desktop, saw the challenge in his eyes and stiffened her spine.

All the same, it took her a few moments to compose her mental processes. Because it had been one thing to think dark thoughts about this man in his absence, but being confronted by him, and suddenly able to see what Daisy had obviously seen in him, made it a slightly different matter.

He wasn't, as she'd expected, to-die-for handsome. On first impressions, that was. She found herself amending the thought. He had thick, straight sandy-brown hair, hazel eyes, a smattering of freckles, and golden hairs glinted on his arms beneath the rolled up sleeves of his khaki bush shirt as a mote of sunlight came in through the skylight. He wore his bush shirt with blue jeans and brown desert boots.

So what was it? Well, he was tall enough—tall enough even for her. Lean, yes, but with wide shoulders, well-knit…

A smile touched her mouth as she wondered exactly what that meant. If it meant all in proportion, with a well-balanced look and the hint of smooth, easy strength beneath his outline, that was exactly the impression Joe Jordan gave. But he was also—interesting, she decided. In a way that was hard to define. You couldn't help gaining the impression that here was a man it could be exciting to know, especially if you were a woman…

She shook her head, reminded herself of his offer to take her to bed although they'd only just met—her blue eyes blazed at the memory—and said, 'We all know how clever you are, Mr. Jordan. One of the better known cartoonists in the country, but—'

'Why would you hold that against me, assuming it's true?'

'Because you have the ability to make people look stupid?' she countered sweetly.

'Only when they deserve it,' he responded mildly.

'Ah, but who's to say your judgement of whether they deserve it or not is always accurate?'

Joe Jordan frowned and sat forward. 'Have I offended someone you know?'

'No. But you can't deny it would be possible.' Lydia gazed at him seriously.

He shoved a hand through his brown hair, leaving it standing up in spikes. 'And that's cause to disapprove of me in regard to your sister?' he queried sardonically.

'That's cause for *me* to have reservations about you, Mr Jordan,' Lydia said precisely. 'It's your playboy reputation I fear in regard to my sister. Can you deny that you're often seen escorting beautiful women around?'

'Lydia, you wouldn't be a tad jealous of your very lovely and feminine sister, by any chance?' he asked smoothly. 'This—' he gestured towards her, managing to convey that she wasn't particularly feminine '—has the taint of sour grapes about it, if you'll forgive me for saying so.'

Lydia smiled with genuine amusement. 'Not in the slightest, Joe! I hope that doesn't disappoint you. But the fact of the matter is, my sister has plans that you may be unaware of, plans that might not feature on your agenda at all.'

'Such as marriage plans,' he said wearily. 'Look, I can—' But he stopped at the sudden look of searing contempt in Lydia's eyes.

'You can—take care of yourself?' she suggested gently. 'I'm sure you can.'

'Bloody hell,' he muttered, and rubbed his jaw. 'Daisy and I have made no commitments whatsoever, Miss Kelso,' he added. 'So if you're imagining I've led her up the garden path, you're wrong,' he finished flatly, then frowned. 'Isn't she your *older* sister?'

'Daisy is twenty-nine going on nineteen. I'm twenty-six. What you may not understand, Mr Jordan, and I can't blame you for this, is...' Lydia paused and wondered how best to explain.

'Do go on, I'm agog,' he murmured with considerable irony.

'OK. Our father is a poet. Our mother, a pianist, died when we were little and we were raised by an aunt. She's my father's sister and she's a sculptress—'

'An artistic family,' Joe Jordan commented, looking only one step away from utter boredom as he doodled desultorily. 'Daisy plays the violin—I can't wait to find out what you do, Miss Lydia Kelso! Wrestle the double bass?'

'Oh, I'm quite different,' Lydia said flippantly. 'I'm a vet.'

She had the satisfaction of seeing sheer surprise in his hazel eyes. He said slowly, now looking at her rather intently, 'So? Where does all this lead?'

'I'm the only one of the family who is not in the least artistic and happens to have her feet planted squarely on the ground.'

'Are you saying your whole family is mad?' He blinked at her.

'Not at all. But I can't deny they can be quite—eccentric and naive at times, then madly passionate at others, and, well, given in those moments to doing some rash things. Otherwise they're warm and wonderful and I would kill rather than see them get hurt.' Lydia folded her hands in her lap and looked at him serenely.

'What...' Joe Jordan could have killed himself for the slightly nervous way he said the word '...um—rashness has Daisy concocted towards me? I gather that *is* the problem?'

Lydia smiled at him. 'At least you're quick on the uptake, Mr Jordan. I'll tell you. She's decided to have your baby, with or without the benefit of wedlock.'

Joe Jordan's jaw dropped involuntarily, although he

snapped it shut immediately. But before he could utter the cynicism he was prompted towards—*I've heard that one before!*—Lydia went on.

'At the moment she's rather in favour of *out of wedlock*, I have to tell you. I think she looks at herself and sees Jodie Foster, Madonna—there are quite a few famous single mums around—and when you're as devoted to your career as Daisy is, it's certainly easier if you only have a child to worry about. She also adores kids, and although twenty-nine is not old, she's not getting any younger.'

'Why me?' Joe Jordan asked faintly, after a long pause.

Lydia smiled quite warmly at him this time. 'You should feel complimented. She's gone into it very seriously, so she tells me, and she feels that you may contribute the brains she—not exactly lacks, but you're obviously *very* clever.'

Joe Jordan stood up and planted his fists on the desk. 'I said this before but—bloody hell! So that's why she suggested going to bed when...' He let the sentence hang unfinished in the air, and had to suffer Lydia Kelso looking at him with obvious sympathy—something that annoyed him all the more. 'Are you sure you're not making all this up?' he said then, through his teeth.

'Quite sure.'

'What if I did decide to marry her?'

'I'd be only too relieved, Mr Jordan,' Lydia said sincerely. 'Provided you love her, of course. She really needs someone to look after her, especially if she has a child, and I can't always be there. You know, she'd make a wonderful wife.'

'How can you say that?' he demanded bitterly. 'You've just led me to believe she's as mad as a March

Hare! Something the whole Kelso clan could suffer from, if I'm not mistaken, despite your assertion to the contrary,' he added pointedly.

'Look,' Lydia responded coolly, 'it's not that I approve, necessarily, but it's a choice a lot of women are making—and not because they're mad but because they deem it a viable option in today's society, where women can aspire to having careers and continuing to have them instead of retreating to the kitchen sink once they start a family.'

'Go on,' he ordered tersely.

She shrugged. 'Some can cope with it, but I don't think Daisy would be one of them. And, whilst a lot of mistakes you make in the heat of the moment can be corrected, a fatherless child is not one of them.'

Joe Jordan sat down, propped his chin in his hands and considered that this rangy twenty-six-year-old girl knew how to pack her punches. She shot from the hip and was unusually mature, perhaps. 'You said you didn't necessarily approve—apart from Daisy. Why not?'

'I happen to believe a child needs both its parents. Of course it can't always be helped, as in my own case. And it's not that being a natural parent makes one automatically a *perfect* parent. But at least if you have kinship with a child it has to help.'

Joe raised his eyebrows thoughtfully. 'It so happens I agree with you. Nor would I countenance being used as a stud. Do you happen to know whether Daisy intended to put me in the picture? Or did she plan to disappear out of my life with a little bundle of joy I was never to know about?'

'It's the one thing that's causing her a bit of a problem,' Lydia said gravely. 'Well, there are two. While she feels she may be in love with you, she can't be sure that you are with her. If you were, then I'm sure she'd abandon all this nonsense.'

'I'm speechless,' Joe Jordan remarked with considerable feeling.

'Would you like to tell me exactly what you do feel for Daisy?' Lydia suggested.

'No! That is,' he corrected himself irritably and ironically, 'I have no intention of marrying her. I have to be honest. Or *anyone* at the moment,' he said moodily. 'But—look, this has been a light-hearted—I couldn't even call it an affair. She was the one who...dammit!' He glared at Lydia.

'Well, now you know why. But you must have liked her? Or do you pop into bed with every woman who indicates they're willing?' She eyed him innocently.

He swore, seriously this time.

Lydia waited, looking absolutely unruffled.

He gritted his teeth. 'I like her. She's fun to be with, she's extremely decorative, but...' He groped for the right words, then sighed savagely.

'You don't miss her when she's not there?'

He narrowed his eyes. 'Is that a true test? You sound as if you...know what you're talking about.'

'I got married when I was twenty,' Lydia said quietly. 'We had a year together before he was drowned in a boating accident. That's how it happened for me. He was always on my mind. Tucked into the background at times, yes, but always there.'

Joe Jordan swallowed visibly and looked discomforted.

Lydia went on before he could formulate any words. 'Please don't feel you need to apologise for anything you may have implied. Nor did I tell you to make you uncomfortable—'

'Then why?' he interrupted. 'And how come you use your maiden name?'

Lydia stood up. 'My husband's name was also Kelso, although we were not related at all. It was one of those strange coincidences because it's not very common. As to why I told you—it was to establish my credibility, I guess. This is not sour grapes, and I do have some experience in these matters.'

'So what do you suggest I do?' He lay back and eyed her narrowly.

'I'll leave that up to you, Mr Jordan. But if you do what I think you intend to—let her down lightly, please.'

'I gather you'll be there to pick up any pieces?'

Lydia hesitated briefly. 'I'm just about to start a position on a cattle station. It's only temporary—I'm filling in for a friend while he takes leave—so, no. However, my father and my aunt are in residence at present. Now, my father,' she said, with a faint smile touching her mouth, 'may not be quite as civilised as I've been should Daisy be inconsolable.'

Joe Jordan stood up with disbelief written in every line of his face. 'Is that a threat?'

'Oh, I don't think he'd do you any bodily harm. But he might come and harangue you, that kind of thing.'

'I don't believe this!' He thumped his fist on the desk, then doubled up in pain clutching his shoulder.

Lydia blinked, then moved around the desk with her boyish stride. 'Can I help?'

'No, you can't! I'm a human being. Why would I need a bloody vet?'

Of course it was surprise, he figured out, that had allowed him to be overpowered by a woman. Mind you, he told himself, she was quite strong, even unusually strong, because he'd ended up back in his chair with her long, capable hands massaging and gently manipulating his neck and shoulder in a way that brought him almost instant relief.

'How did it happen?' she asked conversationally.

He sighed. 'I was playing tennis and pulled a muscle. Just takes time, so they say. How…you did tell me you were a vet, didn't you?' he enquired bitterly.

Lydia laughed down into his upturned face. 'Animals also have muscles, tendons and nerves. I specialise in horses and I've done quite a lot of work with racehorses and polo ponies; they often pull muscles. There. What you need is regular physiotherapy, probably.'

She moved round to stand in front of him and held out her hand.

Joe Jordan didn't take it immediately for the very good reason that he was suddenly struck by the insane desire to see this girl without her clothes. To unbutton her mannish jacket and watch the pinstriped trousers sink to the floor, to find out how her figure was curved and how she could be strong yet so slim, to watch that fascinating stride…

'Goodbye, Mr Jordan,' she said gravely. 'I feel we understand each other quite well, don't you?'

If you can understand going from one sister to the other. If you have any idea how enigmatic you appear, Lydia Kelso. If you can understand that you've successfully made me feel like a piece of horseflesh… He bit his lip on all that was hovering on the tip of his tongue and said instead, 'I guess so. Goodbye, Miss Kelso. You have magic hands, by the way.'

'So I'm told. Oh!'

He followed her dark blue gaze to see it resting on his sketchpad. 'Ah, I apologise,' he murmured. 'I do these things without thinking sometimes.'

But Lydia was laughing down at the cartoon of herself, immensely tall and obviously haranguing a diminutive, seated Joe Jordan in short pants, whose feet didn't even touch the ground. 'It's so good,' she said, still chuckling appreciatively.

'It's not meant to make *you* laugh,' he replied with dignity.

'Then I must have an odd sense of humour! May I have it?' She paused, then added blithely, 'I can use it to warn myself against being too dictatorial and overpowering, even bossy.'

'You don't believe that for one moment, do you?' he countered.

She laughed again. 'How could you tell?'

He paused. 'I just have the feeling you...' He hesitated, and wondered what use it was to ponder any further about Daisy Kelso's surprising sister. 'Oh, well, it doesn't matter, I guess.' But as he stood up he was curiously relieved to discover he was an inch taller than she was.

'No. It doesn't,' she agreed, with an oddly significant little glance.

He shook her hand, then tore the drawing off the pad and gave it to her.

'I'll get it framed—don't bother to come down; I'll let myself out,' she murmured, with a look of delicious mischief in her eyes now. And she went round the desk, slung her navy bag on her shoulder and strode out.

She was still chuckling as she walked along the street in Balmain where Joe Jordan had his townhouse. It was a lovely afternoon and, since its revival in the 1960s, Balmain was a pleasant spot.

One of Sydney's oldest suburbs, on a peninsula into

the harbour with a few miles of coastline, its fortunes had been varied. But although there were plenty of interesting and historic buildings from its early times of affluence, it now had a trendy population, and she wouldn't mind a townhouse there herself, she thought, as she waited for the ferry to take her across the harbour. Especially one as nicely restored as Joe Jordan's.

But then, he could be described as trendy himself, she mused, which she was not, particularly, yet he wasn't *quite* what she'd expected...

The ferry came and she stepped aboard and turned to have a last look not only at Balmain but at the home suburb of, yes, she had to admit it, a slightly intriguing man.

That evening, as she was putting the finishing touches to her packing, Daisy wandered into her room and sat down at the dressing table.

'I'm going to miss you, Lyd,' she said as she unpinned the glorious fall of her dark hair and started to brush it.

'Me too.' Lydia sat down on the bed and eyed her sister's back. 'But you'll have plenty to occupy yourself, what with the Musica Viva tour and the start of the symphony season.'

Daisy sighed and lowered her hand. 'Can't seem to get excited about it, somehow.' She swung round on the stool. 'It's my biological clock,' she added. 'I can feel it ticking away madly.'

'It actually ticks?'

Daisy pulled a face. 'You know what I mean. I just wish,' she said intensely, 'you could meet Joe and give me your opinion. Then I'd know whether to go ahead or not.'

Lydia experienced an inner tremor of guilt, but she

said easily, 'There's an old saying—when in doubt, do nowt. To be honest, Daisy, I think you should put up with your biological clock a bit longer and wait for the right man to come along.'

'So you've said. But you're not twenty-nine—I'll be thirty in two months!'

'Maybe you're confusing the dreaded thirty—remember when we used to think anyone over thirty was ancient?—with the biological clock?'

Daisy smiled briefly. 'I just keep thinking my life is slipping away from me, and that there may not be a Mr Right out there for me.'

'So Joe,' Lydia said carefully, 'is not necessarily Mr Right?'

'Joe's lovely, most of the time. He can also be moody and sarcastic, and there are times when I don't think he knows I exist.'

Lydia smoothed a pair of khaki shorts across her lap as she wondered how to ask her sister whether she'd actually slept with Joe Jordan. This was one point Daisy had been reticent about, but then she was always reticent, if not to say capable of closing up like a clam, with her family on this touchy subject, because they, above all, knew how frequently she fell in and out of love. But would Joe Jordan squire around a beautiful woman he was not sleeping with? A woman who had indicated her willingness on their first date? She doubted it deeply, Lydia decided.

She asked cautiously instead, 'Would you say you're having an affair with him, Daisy?'

'Not *exactly*. I mean, when I decided I wanted him for the father of my child, I made most of the running, you could say. Then I thought—Hey, this guy is also something else; he can give you goosebumps just by looking at you, let alone the rest of it, so…' She paused with an uplifted expression on her face that Lydia felt answered her question better than words might. 'So,' Daisy went on, 'then I thought, Perhaps I should hang on to him but, put simply, Lyd, he's not that easy to hang on to.'

Daisy's eyes were a true violet. She wasn't tall, she had a perfect oval face, a lovely figure, she was exquisitely groomed, even for a dinner at home, and she looked every inch a sophisticated twenty-nine-year-old. Nor did her just uttered sentiments belie this—unless you knew her well enough to know that of the two of them she was the much more naive.

'Does he have other women?' Lydia asked, packing her shorts and reaching for a blouse.

'I don't think so. But the fact of the matter is he hasn't had much of me lately. He's losing interest, I would say.'

Thank heavens, Lydia thought. She said bracingly, 'Then he's not worth it, Daisy. Besides, you could end up with a moody kid!'

'All the same, there's something about him—'.

'Listen, Daisy.' Lydia was suddenly serious. 'I went along with this when I thought you were theorizing as opposed to actually doing it, because you're a lot like Dad. Once he gets an idea into his mind nothing can change it until he gets it out of his system.'

'Thank you,' Daisy said gravely.

'But now it's time for straight talking,' Lydia went on pointedly. 'If you love Joe Jordan and he loves you and wants to marry you, you have my blessing. Otherwise it's a dangerous game you're playing—don't do this to yourself. You're worth much more than a life of seducing men so you can have a baby.'

Daisy turned the brush over in her hands. 'You don't know what it's like, Lyd,' she said slowly. 'You fell in love once and it worked out perfectly—well, until Brad died, of course. But it never works perfectly for me.' She brushed away a tear.

'Could you be…could you be a shade too generous, Daisy?' Lydia suggested, picking her words with care. 'Why don't you play hard to get for a change?'

Daisy lifted her head as if struck by inspiration. 'Oh. Maybe Joe would respond to that!'

'Forget Joe Jordan—' Lydia broke off and bit her lip. 'Why?'

'Uh—you told me yourself that he's very clever and that he can be moody and sarcastic. That's always hard to live with unless you're clever in the same way. What you need is someone musical, someone who could share the area where you're really sensitive and creative.'

Daisy stared reflectively into the distance. 'There is a new oboe player who's just joined the orchestra. He's rather sweet, and I can tell he's interested, but, no, it wouldn't work.'

'It's probably far too early to tell whether it would work,' Lydia commented practically, 'but how can you be so sure it wouldn't?'

'He's younger.'

'Younger… How much?'

'He's about your age, I guess.'

Lydia was struck silent for a long moment, struck by the irony of her sister plotting to have some man's child to bring up on her own yet unable to contemplate a normal relationship with a man because he was a little younger…

She said, at length, 'Three years—that's nothing, really.'

'Oh, yes, it is. When I'm thirty he'll still be in his twenties. More importantly, when I'm fifty, he'll still be in his forties. I'm sure it should be the other way around because men tend to age better than women, don't you think?'

But Lydia was suddenly gripped by the feeling that a younger man could be just what Daisy needed. Might it not bring out a so far latent streak of maturity in her? As well as getting her over Joe Jordan, of course. Then she sighed and decided she'd done enough interfering in her sister's life for one day.

'Why don't you just wait and see what happens?' she murmured, and reached for the silver-framed photo of Brad on the dressing table. She stared down at it, blinked a couple of times, then laid it gently face down on top of her clothes in the suitcase.

Daisy was on her feet in a flash, and she knelt in front of Lydia and took her hands. 'Do you still miss him so much, darling? I had hoped it was getting easier.'

'It is, mostly,' Lydia said tremulously. 'Just sometimes it's actually harder. I don't know why. Unless it's because I'm afraid I'll forget.'

'You know,' her sister said, 'you worry an awful lot about me, but I can tell you that Brad loved you so much he would not want you to be unhappy for ever. And it's been five years now. Time to stop living a half-life. Time to have no guilt about finding someone else.'

Lydia smiled painfully. 'The problem is, I couldn't care less if I never did find anyone else. Men don't seem to interest me much, apart from—' She stopped abruptly as it surfaced in her mind that Joe Jordan was the first interesting man she'd met for a long time. To make matters worse, she'd been just about to say it.

'So there is someone?' Daisy said eagerly.

'No!' Lydia denied hastily.

'But you said—"apart from..."'?

'Um—the ones you can't have,' Lydia improvised madly, then thought, Well, that wasn't so far from the truth either.

'Still, that could be a start!' Daisy frowned. 'Anyone I know?'

'No. No—'

'Is he married?' Daisy asked, with both understanding and sympathy. 'A lot of the best ones are.'

'You're right—was that Chattie calling?' Their aunt Charlotte was universally known as Chattie Kelso, and she still lived with them in the big old house at Bronte, a beachside suburb of Sydney where both Daisy and Lydia had grown up.

Daisy rose. 'She's cooked roast pork,' she said conspiratorially. 'You know how paranoid she is about getting the crackling crisp. We'd better not keep her waiting.'

James Kelso, who was renowned for his bush ballads and poetry written under the name of Kelso James, as well as renowned for always wearing a bush shirt and jeans, raised his glass and cleared his throat. 'I'd like to propose several toasts. First to you, my dear Chattie, for the crispest crackling you've ever produced.'

Chattie, a spinster in her fifties, with Lydia's colouring and build although her hair was sprinkled with grey now, looked gratified. She raised her glass in return and her fine eyes glinted with mischief. 'Thought so myself, although I didn't like to say it.'

'And to you, my dear Daisy—' James inclined his head towards his elder daughter '—for looking sensational, as usual. No one would think you were a day over nineteen.'

Daisy smiled fondly at him. 'Dad, you're sweet, but you tell awful lies!'

'May one enquire how your love life is going at present?'

'One may—it's going, but it's at a critical stage, you could say.'

'Hmm. Dangerous age, twenty-nine. Would you agree, Chattie?'

'No. They can all be dangerous. I consider myself at my most dangerous when I was seventeen, closely followed by thirty-nine. At seventeen I would have done anything to have a boyfriend and be like the rest of the girls, and at thirty-nine I would have done anything to have a husband.'

'What about children?' Daisy asked.

'That too. I gave serious thought to having one without a husband—'

'Chattie!' James reproved. 'Don't put silly ideas into their young heads.'

Lydia ate her roast pork and thought that if Joe Jordan were a fly on the wall he might be able to judge for himself how eccentric her family could be.

'If you'd let me finish,' Chattie said, 'I decided against it because I realised it was extremely unfair to a child to deprive it of a father.'

Lydia put her knife and fork down and glanced at her aunt through her lashes. Had a whiff of Daisy's state of mind got through to her?

'I have to agree,' James said. 'For example, do you or do you not think I've enriched your lives, girls?'

Daisy masked her expression almost immediately, but Lydia saw her sheer horror at the thought of never having known their father, and she felt like cheering at the same time as she wondered whether her father had also divined Daisy's dilemma...

She said, 'Dad, you've not only enriched our lives but your wisdom never ceases to amaze me—when you're not driving me mad with your forgetfulness, your inability to find your glasses, even when they're on top of your head, and the way you persistently wear odd socks—when you remember to wear them at all.'

'Well, that brings me to you, Lydia, my younger and most practical daughter,' James said humorously. 'We're going to miss you, my dear. Who else will we have to fix fuses and start our cars when they break down? You know how hopeless I am at that kind of thing.'

'I do.' Lydia grinned. 'Heaven alone knows where that expertise came down to me from, but if you just look in the *Yellow Pages* you'll find there are electricians, mechanics, plumbers and so on galore—on second thoughts, I'd better write you out a list.'

'Now that makes us feel really small,' James Kelso admonished, 'but I'd be much easier if you did! And I know I speak for the rest of us when I say we're all happy to think of you enjoying a new challenge, a new experience—may it be a wonderful one!' He raised his glass again.

'Hear, hear!' Chattie and Daisy echoed.

'So let's think up a suitable limerick,' James went on.

It was a game they'd played ever since Lydia could remember...

'*Lydia Kelso is going to Queensland,*' Daisy started.

'*To...look after cows...with a magic hand,*' Chattie supplied.

'*Not for too long,*' James said.

'*You won't know I'm gone!*' Lydia laughed.

There was silence until Daisy said frustratedly, 'The last line is always the hardest! What rhymes with Queensland? We've got hand...'

'Wedding band?' Chattie suggested.

'Oh, no!' Lydia protested. 'There's not the least likelihood of that happening, and anyway, I didn't like to interrupt the creative flow, but I'm actually going to the Northern Territory.'

Everyone groaned. 'Oh, well,' James murmured, 'that's right next door, so we won't start again—and you never know! So... *And she'll come home complete with a wedding band.*'

'Very amateurish,' Lydia said. 'But thank you all for your good wishes!' And she looked round the dining room, with its heavy old oak table, dark green walls, examples of her aunt's sculpting and some lovely gold-framed paintings on the wall. 'I'll miss you,' she added. 'Just promise me you'll all be good!'

It struck her as she got ready for bed that she could go away with a much easier mind, now. A quiet word with Chattie had revealed that she was aware of Daisy's dilemma and would keep a weather eye out for her.

'We won't tell your father,' she'd said. 'He's liable to go and want to have things out with this Joe Jordan.'

Lydia had confessed that she'd already done that, but that Daisy was unaware of her actions.

'What's he like?' Chattie had asked curiously.

'Interesting, but not serious about her—nor, I suspect, did he stand much chance. She made the running, so to speak.'

'So she is sleeping with him?'

'She hasn't actually admitted to that, but she looks, well, you know...'

'I do. But he could have knocked her back. How like a man!'

They'd looked at each other, then grinned simultaneously.

'Daisy, in full flight, is a sight to behold,' Chattie had acknowledged. 'Perhaps I was being a bit hard on him. What about you?'

Lydia had blinked. 'What about me?'

'When are you going to lay Brad to rest and start living again?'

'Not you too!'

'Your father been giving you a hard time?'

Lydia had shaken her head. 'Daisy. But I am living, and enjoying myself and really looking forward to this job!'

'All right.' Chattie had looked as if she'd been about to say more, but had desisted and hugged her niece instead. 'Leave them to me; I'll look after them!'

Lydia took off her pinstriped trouser suit, donned a velvet housecoat and sat down at her dressing table to brush her hair, after removing a few very dark strands from the brush.

She'd returned to this room and this single bed after a year of marriage, and some days it was hard to believe she'd ever left it.

She and Brad had met at university, he'd been studying economics, and the first thing to draw them together had been their common although unusual surname. But the attraction had been almost instantaneous, and mutual. It had also been a revelation to Lydia, because he'd been her first serious boyfriend, and to find someone she clicked with so completely had been totally unexpected.

To fall so much in love when she'd expected to spend

her university years working hard to achieve her career goals had also been disconcerting, but that had been another wonderful part of their relationship. They'd been quite happy to allow each other the space to study.

So, after two years, and before she had graduated—although he had, and had joined an eminent firm of stockbrokers—they'd got married, got themselves a small flat and had a year of idyllic happiness.

It had been a matter of surprise to many, her family included, that she should have been the first sister to marry, and so young.

He'd been such fun, she thought sadly, the night before she went—not to Queensland, although via it to the Northern Territory. Not that you'd necessarily have known that behind his glasses and his computer-like brain there had lurked a delicious sense of humour. And he'd handled her growing ardour with surprising passion for a man who had always been able to tell you how many points the All Ordinaries or the Dow Jones had gained or dropped overnight.

It wasn't fair. She'd thought it so many times, when her body had ached physically for him, and her mind had yearned for the warmth, tenderness and laughter they'd generated together.

She'd also suffered the growing conviction it would never happen for her that way again. So that, despite their good intentions, she hated it when people told her it was time to think of falling in love again—even her own sister.

She brushed steadily for a few minutes, trying to compose herself, and finally found some relief from her sad thoughts coming from an unusual direction...Joe Jordan and his hints that she was not as feminine as her gorgeous sister.

She put the brush down and studied herself in the mirror. What would he have thought, she mused, if he'd known that under her suit she'd been wearing—these?

'These', beneath her velvet robe, were a midnight-blue silk camisole deeply edged with lace and a matching pair of panties.

She stood up, opened her robe and, putting her hands on her hips, twirled slowly in front of the mirror. True, she conceded to her image, she was not like Daisy, who had an hourglass figure, but—how had Brad put it? Beneath her clothes she was slim, sleek and surprisingly sensuous, and her legs were to die for.

Of course, she told herself as she sat down again and grinned at herself, what appeals to one man may not appeal to another! And although her clothes were sometimes mannish it was only for comfort, and they were beautifully made. She also had a passion for shoes and bags and the finest lingerie.

So there, Mr Jordan, she thought, and was tempted to stick out her tongue at a mental image of him.

Then she sobered and wondered what on earth she was thinking. Only minutes ago she'd been consumed by sadness and the unfairness of fate—how could she be thinking of another man? A man her sister might be in love with—might even have slept with, moreover.

She closed her eyes and clenched her hands until Brad came back to her in her mind, and she remembered how he'd loved to cook, but had been quite hopeless at clearing up after himself...

CHAPTER TWO

SEVERAL days later she was winging her way to Katerina Station in the Victoria River District of the Northern Territory, five hundred kilometres south of Darwin. She'd flown first to Townsville, to spend two days with Brad's parents in North Queensland, then on to Darwin to spend a day in the veterinary science department of the Northern Territory University.

The vet she was filling in for, although not precisely as a vet, was a friend from university, Tim Patterson. They'd kept in touch over the years, and several months ago he'd written to tell her that he was taking a break from his practice and doing something he'd always wanted to do—joining a mustering team on a cattle station where not only his horsemanship but his veterinary expertise would be useful.

Then, a few weeks ago, he'd written again to say that he was having the time of his life mustering cattle, that it was also wonderful experience for a vet interested in large animals, but for business and personal reasons he needed to take six weeks off and would she be interested in filling in for him? He'd assured her that the Simpson family, who ran Katerina Station, would welcome her enthusiastically and provide accommodation for her in the main homestead—when she wasn't sleeping under the stars with the rest of the mustering team.

That had done it. She'd gone, cap in hand, to the senior partner of the practice she was working for in Sydney and showed him the letter. He'd given her six weeks' leave and added enviously, 'Half your luck, Lydia!'

She was now staring down at the grassy plains, rolling savanna and rocky outcrops of the Victoria River District, known locally as the VRD, as it glided past below. It was a fine, clear day and the sky was huge, so was the panorama beneath it, giving Lydia a sense of the vastness and the emptiness of the ancient continent she called home.

The VRD supported one of the most successful grazing enterprises in northern Australia, but to look down upon it you wouldn't think a soul lived in it.

The station pilot was young and friendly, and he smiled at her wonderment and took an extra ten minutes to show her the various sets of cattle yards and bores as proof that cattle did exist in large numbers, then he buzzed the Katerina homestead to alert the occupants of his imminent arrival.

He also filled her in about the Simpson family. 'Sarah is a daughter of the pioneering family that started Katerina,' he explained. 'She and her brother inherited it, but when she married she divided her share with her husband, Rolf, and he actually manages the place.'

'What about the brother?' Lydia asked.

'He spends time here, he's still the major shareholder, but he doesn't live here—look, there's a mob on the way to the main yards.'

Lydia stared down at the dust being raised by a mob of cattle as they were moved along by horsemen.

'Do you only muster by horseback?' she asked. 'I thought most of it was done by chopper these days.'

'Used to be, for a time, but the ringer's coming back into fashion nowadays. You can't educate a bunch of cows from a chopper.'

'Does that mean you'll be out of a job?' He'd already told her he piloted a Bell 45 helicopter too.

'Nope! We work in conjunction. Choppers still have their uses in really difficult terrain and for moving large mobs. OK, here we go.'

He set the light plane down on a grass airstrip in what looked like the middle of nowhere until a large shed came into view.

Lydia emerged as the dust settled. She breathed deeply and looked around. Tim had confided that being a vet did not necessarily confer any special status on a member of this mustering team. They did most of their vet work themselves, and how you rode and handled cattle was the prime consideration—although some of the bigger stations did employ vets as vets.

She'd found this amusing, because he'd also told her that Katerina Station covered a million acres. What was big if not that? she'd pondered. But he'd gone on to say that once they'd realised you knew what you were talk-ing about and doing, you'd find them deferring to you. So, she would have to prove herself first, she reflected. It would be a nice kind of challenge.

She turned as she heard a vehicle approaching, ex-pecting either Sarah or Rolf Simpson. But as another cloud of dust started to subside as it skidded to a stop beside her, a pale gold Labrador dog leapt off the back of the battered utility and raced towards her, only to sit down in front of her and extend a paw.

'Hello!' Lydia squatted down in front of the dog and shook the paw gravely. 'And who might you be? I have to tell you I think you're gorgeous, and so well-mannered.'

The dog grinned widely and a voice above Lydia said,

'Glad you approve of my dog. OK, Meg, back in the ute.'

Meg obeyed, but not before giving the owner of the voice a loving lick as he put his hand down to her.

Lydia straightened dazedly. Because there was no mistaking that voice, nor any chance of mistaking the tall man standing in front of her, although he looked so different from the last time she'd seen him.

'What the hell are you doing here?' It came out before she could help herself as she took in the stained, dusty clothes he wore and the battered felt cowboy hat he dangled—none of which diminished the impact of that 'well-knit' tall body and 'interesting' face beneath his brown hair...

'Good morning to you, Miss Lydia Kelso—or rather Mrs,' Joe Jordan drawled, and leant casually against the bonnet of the vehicle as he allowed his hazel gaze to run over the olive-green stretch moleskins and cream shirt she wore with a sleeveless quilted olive vest and brown boots. Her hair was tousled, but he couldn't imagine it any other way, he found himself thinking, and it was a gloriously free head of hair, that framed those delicate features admirably.

Lydia, on the other hand, shook her tousled head and looked around, blinking experimentally. 'Am I on Katerina Station in the Northern Territory run by the Simpson family, or have I been kidnapped?' she queried.

'Not at all—'

'So how did you get here from Balmain?'

'As I was about to explain, Sarah Simpson is my sister,' he said mildly.

'You're the brother who owns half of the place?' Lydia stared at him incredulously.

'None other. I don't usually trade on it,' he added modestly, 'but after you left me the other day, I suddenly thought to myself—Didn't Rolf let me know that Tim had to go away for six weeks but he'd found someone to take his place who also happened to be a vet? My next thought was that it would be an interesting coincidence should you be the person replacing him.'

'I'm speechless,' Lydia said, in a parody of what he'd said to her three days ago.

Joe Jordan straightened. 'You weren't exactly speechless the other day.'

Lydia gestured futilely. 'So what are you doing here now?'

'Decided to come up for a bit of R&R at the same time as I check out how the new vet handles herself, amongst other things.'

Lydia muttered something beneath her breath.

'That doesn't recommend itself to you?' he asked, with the most wicked spark of mischief in his eyes.

'No, it does not. You're the last person I want peering over my shoulder all the time!'

'Now why would that be?' he asked ingenuously. 'I thought anything taking me out of reach of your sister would meet with your approval.'

Lydia stared at him. 'Because the circumstances in which we met were not exactly auspicious,' she said deliberately. 'And did you just walk out on my sister?'

His eyes glinted with irony now. 'As a matter of fact, no. I told her that I had to be out of town for a while.'

'Was she devastated?' Lydia demanded.

'If so she gave no hint of it. I had actually prepared a sort of—not exactly farewell address, but a letting-down-lightly kind of thing, as you so thoughtfully recommended—only it never got said because she took the words right out of my mouth. She said that she thought it would be an excellent idea if we had a bit of a break from each other.'

Lydia digested this, then swore beneath *her* breath this time.

'Which indicated to me,' Joe Jordan said, with a wryly raised eyebrow, 'that she's losing interest in me and the idea of me fathering her child.'

No, she's not, she's playing hard to get!

Lydia didn't say it, she bit the words off on the tip of her tongue, but she experienced a sinking feeling in the pit of her stomach that generally indicated she was right about her lovely sister Daisy's state of mind.

'I can't believe this,' she said instead. 'I was really looking forward to this experience.'

He frowned. 'Surely my simple presence couldn't provide that much of a blight?'

'Your presence is not simple at all,' she retorted.

He stared at her thoughtfully. 'Does that mean you were rather intrigued about me, as I discovered I was about you, dear Lydia?' he queried.

She'd never been a blusher, but she undoubtedly coloured. She could feel the heat of it beneath the smooth skin of her cheeks and down her neck, all of which he noted with a flicker of amusement twisting his lips.

It was his amusement that got her going again, when she really would have loved to crawl into a handy hole to hide. 'How *could* you—apart from anything else— transfer from one sister to another just like…clicking your fingers?' She demonstrated, and he laughed openly this time.

'Funnily enough, I asked myself that,' he murmured. 'The only conclusion I could come up with was that your sister had singled me out from the herd, slightly against my better judgement, whereas *you* and I...came together differently.'

'We didn't,' she protested. 'We came together—we *met*—because of my sister!'

'Whatever.' He waved a negligent hand. 'This interest we share, however, sprang up of its own accord. Daisy had nothing to do with it.'

'I'm not admitting to...' She bit her lip and suffered a moment of dread that she would blush again, but she didn't. 'I am not interested in you, Mr Jordan. Let's put it like that.' She stared at him defiantly.

'I would have said your first assertion was more truthful, Lydia. The one about not admitting things. But let's not get ourselves all tied up here and now. Pete's got your gear off the plane. Would you allow me to drive you up to the homestead? Sarah has lunch waiting.'

Lydia was sorely tempted to press her point, if not to find some way of driving it home with a sledgehammer, but she contained herself and only looked supremely frustrated.

Joe Jordan watched her for a moment, then said, 'Good. I wouldn't have believed you anyway, and it's hot enough without getting oneself unnecessarily hot and bothered. After you, ma'am!' He walked round the ute and opened the passenger door for her.

She did say stiffly as they drove away, 'It is hot, for the middle of winter.'

'Ah, but the nights are deliciously cool at this time of year, in comparison. Ever been up this way before, Lydia?'

'No.'

'Then you're in for a delightful surprise. The country is superb at the moment. We had a good wet season, everything's still flourishing, you can get about easily—do you ride?'

'Of course!' She looked at him scathingly, then looked out of the window.

'Excellent. Unless, that is, you intend to converse with me only in monosyllables for the next six weeks?'

She turned back to him wide-eyed. 'You're not going to be here for six whole weeks, are you?'

He shrugged. 'More or less.'

'But why? Surely you don't usually spend so much time up here!'

'How would you know?' he countered.

'I...well, I assumed you lived most of your life in Sydney,' she offered—a shade feebly, she couldn't help thinking.

'As in making generalisations about people from the same family, one shouldn't make assumptions based on very little knowledge of the facts, Lydia,' he reproved gravely.

They were driving along a rocky dirt road towards a stand of tall trees and between them she could see a large tin roof with 'Katerina' painted in big black letters on the silver surface: the roof they'd flown over.

Lydia blinked several times and said tersely, 'I was told you didn't live here.'

'Who told you that?'

'Pete, the pilot. I had no idea, of course, that he was talking about you!'

'Sprung,' Joe Jordan remarked with a charming smile as he wrestled the gear lever and they bounced over a large rock. 'Must get this road fixed, by the way. Uh—no, I don't actually live here, although I spend quite a bit of time up here.'

Lydia waited, then said pointedly, 'So?'

'Several things have happened, that's all. Rolf and Sarah need a bit of a break. Modern technology means that I can still pursue my chosen career from up here, and—well, the other thing that happened may not recommend itself to you, so I might wait.'

'Tell me!' Lydia ordered through her teeth.

He brought the utility to a halt outside a low white pole fence surrounding a lush acre of garden that in turn surrounded the homestead. There were colourful parrots swooping amongst the trees, there was a carpet of thick green grass, the house was old and sprawling, but well maintained, there was a riot of purple, pink and white bougainvillea smothering the tank stands, and a woman standing on the front steps was waving to them.

'All right.' Joe Jordan cut the motor and turned to look at her fully.

He didn't start to speak immediately, however, and, much as she would have wished otherwise, Lydia felt an erratic little frisson run through her at the proximity of this man. Nor was it so hard to define his attractiveness suddenly. It was all there in the lines and angles of his face, the well-cut mouth, those broad shoulders and lean hips, the pair of strong hands, those intelligent hazel eyes, and in the distinct feeling that not only might he be exciting to know, he was also a connoisseur of women.

And he waited until their gazes clashed before he said, 'I've been plagued by the curious yet nevertheless powerful desire to see you without your clothes, Ms Kelso. And the way you walk has taken to invading my thoughts. I do apologise for putting it so plainly, but it is the truth and you did command me to tell you.'

* * *

Lydia washed her hands in the bathroom attached to her bedroom and brushed her hair vigorously.

She'd been welcomed warmly by Sarah Simpson, shown her room and asked if she'd like to brush up before lunch. She hadn't responded to Joe Jordan's statement, beyond bestowing upon him the fieriest of blue glances before she'd jumped out of the utility. It hadn't abashed him in the slightest as he'd introduced her to his sister and brother-in-law.

How on earth she was going to face him over a lunch table and for the next six weeks she had no idea, she mused savagely as she flung her brush down and stood with her hands on her hips. And there was Daisy to think about. Daisy, putting her own advice into practice, unless she was much mistaken.

'Rolf and I have to take a little while off, although it's such a busy time of the year,' Sarah said over lunch.

She was in her early thirties, Lydia judged, with the same colouring as her brother. She was also what one would call 'horsey' but in a not unattractive way. Horses were never far from her conversation, and the verandah room, closed in with glass louvres, where lunch was set out, was decked with ribbons and trophies she'd won for dressage and show jumping, and she wore jodhpurs with a pink blouse.

Another clue to Sarah's preoccupation with horses was that, from what Lydia had seen of the house, and while it was comfortable enough, the furnishings were old-fashioned, and it didn't give off the glow of a dedicated homemaker being in residence.

Sarah had also been boarding-school-educated, and there were photos on the wall depicting a young Sarah Jordan as school captain. She had a rather bracing, authoritative air, as if she were a school captain born and bred. One thing she wasn't, by her own admission, was much of a cook.

Lunch, while plentiful, was plain. Cold meat and salad, a fruit bowl and cheese.

'Do, *do* make free use of the kitchen, Lydia,' she invited. 'I only do the basics, I'm afraid.'

'Watch it,' Joe advised Lydia. 'You could find yourself not only the resident vet but head chef.'

'Just because you got my share of the cooking genes, Joe, there is no need to be smug. We're twins,' Sarah confided to Lydia. 'I sometimes think things got a bit muddled up. I should have got the artistic bent, one feels, but...' She shrugged.

'Hang on, beloved,' Joe advised his sister this time, 'you could be giving the wrong impression here.'

Sarah blinked her hazel eyes at her brother. 'Darling,' she murmured, 'one only has to count the trail of broken hearts you've left amongst the female population of the Territory alone to know otherwise.'

Joe Jordan looked hurt and outraged at the same time. 'Now you've really done it, Sarah!'

'Done what?' She eyed him innocently.

'Lydia already classes me with Casanova!'

Sarah transferred her gaze to Lydia with some interest. 'Joe mentioned that you two know each other. I didn't realise it was in *that* way.'

'It's not,' Lydia replied coolly. 'It's my sister he knows in "that way".'

Rolf Simpson, a man of few words so far—in fact to Lydia he epitomised the fair dinkum cattleman: tall, lean, sparse of speech and with far-seeing blue eyes—said, 'It's never a good idea to come between sisters, mate.'

Lydia flashed a triumphant look at the main shareholder of Katerina Station, then turned her attention to her lunch and the dodging of some uncooked pieces of potato in the salad of the same name.

'I'm suitably chastened; however—' Joe took a draught of his beer '—I didn't seek out either of the Kelso sisters.'

'Gosh!' Sarah enthused. 'We could be in for some interesting times, by the sound of it. I'm almost tempted to put our little holiday off, Rolf. She turned to Lydia. 'I must tell you, if what I think is going on between you two, *is* going on between you two, I should be delighted to have a vet for a sister-in-law. Just think how handy it would be for my horses, let alone Katerina.'

This time it was Joe Jordan who flashed Lydia a look that, while not exactly triumphant, spoke volumes.

'When, exactly, do you plan to take your holiday?' Lydia enquired of Sarah.

'In a fortnight,' Sarah replied. 'We'll be taking three weeks. But Joe'll be here, so it's not as if we're abandoning you!'

'I imagine,' Joe Jordan commented, 'that Lydia doesn't quite see it that way.'

'Why ever not?' Sarah looked perplexed.

'She'll probably tell you herself; she's a plain speaker, our Lydia.'

'Joe, I wish you'd stop talking in riddles,' Sarah protested, then turned her attention to Lydia with a smile. 'You do look awfully young to be a fully qualified vet.'

'Twenty-six, although I agree she looks younger,' her brother commented. 'But I can assure you she's very strong.'

'Ignore him,' Sarah said to Lydia. 'He can be impossible.'

But it was Rolf who changed the subject. 'We are

Brucellosis and TB free in the Territory now, Lydia—
did you know?'

'I...yes!' Lydia murmured, wresting her mind from
his brother-in-law, who was sitting back in his chair with
the most devilish little glint in his hazel eyes.

'What do you want now?' Lydia asked arctically, much
later in the day.

It was after dinner, and she'd spent the rest of the day
with Rolf and Joe, doing a tour of the main yards and
the vet station, and she'd even been able to practise her
science on a lame stock horse. She'd found a nail in its
hoof and been able to extract it.

Neither man had said much during the operation, but
she'd known they were watching keenly. After the nail
had come out, and she'd injected the horse with an an-
tibiotic and a tetanus needle, Rolf had remarked that no
one else had been able to come up with the cause of the
horse's lameness. It had been a way of saying well done,
she gathered.

But instead of going to bed after dinner, despite yawn-
ing several times, she'd pulled on a dark green pullover,
moved a comfortable cane lounger from the verandah
onto the lawn and sunk down in it to watch the millions
of stars overhead. That was how Joe Jordan had found
her.

'Nothing. I thought you'd retired.' He went away and
came back in moments with another chair. 'Mind if I
join you?'

She glanced at him sardonically and shrugged.

'Thank you,' he returned politely. 'Hang on again; I'll
be right back.'

This time he was away for five minutes, and he came
back with a pottery wine cooler supporting a frosted bot-

tle and two glasses. 'Thought you might appreciate some kind of a nightcap. Because Sarah doesn't drink, she forgets others do. And most people drink wine.'

Meg had followed him, and she put her muzzle in Lydia's lap for a pat before lying down at her master's feet.

'I have no intention of drinking half a bottle of wine.'

He pulled the cork from the pocket of his jeans and showed it to her. 'We can drink as much or as little as we like. It's quite a sight, isn't it?' He gestured skywards.

Lydia hesitated, then accepted the glass he'd poured for her and laid her head back. 'You're not wrong.'

'There's only one better way, and that's to be camped out. No tent, just a swag beside a small fire, the horses hobbled not far away.'

'That's the kind of stuff my father writes about,' she said dreamily. 'He was a jackeroo as a young man. He always says it got into his blood.'

'I've read some of his work. It's good. I'm surprised he didn't take you outback.'

'Oh, he did. Just not to the Northern Territory. Cooper Creek, the Barcoo, Lake Eyre—I've seen those.'

There was a long silence; Lydia sipped her wine and made no attempt to break it.

It was Joe who finally said, 'Why are you so mad at me?'

Surprise held her further silent for a moment, then she said wearily, 'I'm not.'

'You could have fooled me, but if we discount Daisy as a possible reason—what's left?'

It was no good trying to study his expression, it was too dark, despite the Milky Way seeming to hang just above their heads, but she had the feeling he was serious.

'You don't really hold being a cartoonist against me?' he queried. 'As you see, it's not the only thing I can do.'

'No…' She sighed.

'And you shouldn't believe Sarah's stories about a trail of broken hearts—'

'Why not?'

He paused. 'Because it's not true. I… Lydia, are you laughing at me, by any chance?' he asked ominously.

She sat up chuckling. 'Yes. Heaven alone knows why, Mr Jordan, but I'm quite sure it *is* true, or was when you were a young man in these parts.'

'What tells you this?'

'You'd probably have to be a woman to understand.'

'It's funny you should say that—I read a quote the other day that intrigued me. On the subject of women.'

'Do tell me,' she invited.

'"Any man smart enough to understand women is also smart enough to keep quiet about it."'

Lydia smiled. 'Do you?'

'Understand women? I would have thought so,' he murmured thoughtfully. 'Until I met you.'

'Oh, come now. This is only the second time we've met, and I've got an early start tomorrow, so…' She drained her glass and handed it to him.

But he merely reached for the bottle on the grass beside him and refilled it. 'One more won't hurt, surely? Besides, I got the feeling it was loosening you up, Ms Kelso.' He put the glass back into her hands.

'Is that how you do it? Ply them with alcohol?'

'Not at all,' he denied. 'But I thought you were uptight, feeling less than restful, and it might help.'

Lydia hesitated, then settled back. 'If you hadn't been

the first person I bumped into on Katerina I might be feeling a lot more restful. If I didn't think my sister Daisy was—' She broke off.

'I told you what happened.'

'I know. You also told me you had this *curious* desire to see me without my clothes. As if I might be some sort of circus freak.' As soon as she'd said it Lydia regretted the words, and was amazed to discover that she had subconsciously taken umbrage at that particular word.

'Ah.' Joe Jordan drained his glass and refilled it. 'That wasn't what I meant at all, but I apologise for phrasing things awkwardly. What I meant was, if I'd thought you were some sort of circus freak, the last thing I'd want is to see you undressed. Do you perceive the difference, Lydia?'

'I perceive that you're getting yourself tangled up in technicalities, Joe! But, no, you don't have to explain further. I know exactly what you meant.'

'You do? Would you be so kind as to tell me what I meant?' he asked, with some chagrin.

Lydia grinned fleetingly. 'That at first you didn't find me feminine and to your taste, especially compared to my sister Daisy. You know, I would have had to be particularly dense not to have got that message loud and clear, Joe.'

She could see enough to see him flinch, and had to laugh softly. 'Look, don't let it come between you and your sleep,' she advised. 'I grew up in Daisy's shadow; I'm quite used to it.'

'And once again I'm speechless.'

'Good,' she said unfeelingly. 'Because I'm getting tired of this conversation and I am going to bed.'

'Mind you, I'm relieved it's not because of some of

the things Sarah said—the other things about mixed up genes and being able to cook,' he said humorously.

'I wouldn't hold that against a man,' Lydia replied. 'My husband was a fantastic cook, although disastrously messy.'

Joe Jordan stared down at the wine glass cradled in his hands, and said at last, 'Is that it, Lydia?'

She stood up in one lithe movement. 'Yes, Joe, that's it. You see, it was so wonderful I…can't forget him or believe it could ever happen that way for me again.'

He stood up, and Meg rose like a wraith in the dark to stand patiently beside him. 'Then Daisy is not part of it?'

'Daisy *is* part of it,' she contradicted. 'If…' She paused and chose her words with care. 'You are at all serious about an interest in me, then you've run into a double whammy, so to speak. My memories of Brad and the impossibility of having anything to do with a man my sister may love. Goodnight.'

This time she took her glass with her as she walked inside.

Joe Jordan sat down again after a moment and took his dog's face into his hands. 'My dear Meg,' he murmured, 'who would have believed I could have been such a fool? Not that I was to know—all sorts of things—but I've been about as heavy-handed as a bull in a china shop—if you'll forgive my mixed metaphors. However, it would be fair to say I'm all the more intrigued. You do like her, don't you?'

Meg gazed lovingly up at him and wagged her tail.

'Good. As they say, tomorrow is another day. And another strategy is obviously called for. We shall see!'

About a week later, Lydia got up at the crack of dawn, then remembered it was a Sunday, so she got back into bed and fell asleep until ten o'clock.

There seemed to be no one about as she padded into the kitchen then and made herself some tea and toast. She took it back to her bedroom and spent the next hour leisurely engaged in doing the things she'd hadn't had much time for over the previous week.

She washed her hair, left the conditioner on and wrapped her head in a towel. She attended to her nails and smoothed moisturiser all over herself at the same time as she checked herself for bruises and saddle sores; there were no sores but a few colourful bruises. She paused to wonder whether her skin and hair would ever be the same again, despite this treatment, and sat down to write a long letter home.

Finally, she unwound the towel, rinsed her hair and dressed in a pair of cool pink linen shorts with a pink and white floral cotton blouse, luxuriating as she did so in clothes that were not khaki or definitely working clothes, and slid a pair of light sandals on.

She wondered again why the homestead was so silent, then shrugged. A week at Katerina had been long enough to discover that one day was very much like another, although she'd been told firmly to take Sundays off. Sarah would most likely be with her horses, and Rolf and Joe, if they weren't working on the road or the cattle yards or the airstrip or the maintenance of some vehicle or another, could still find a hundred other tasks.

She went out onto the verandah and pulled a chair into the sunlight so she could dry her hair, and ran a mental review of the week as she closed her eyes and lifted her face to the sun.

A faint smile curved her lips at the memory of how stiff she'd been for the first few days, and was still stiff at times. This was despite begging a friend in Sydney, as soon as she'd decided to come to Katerina, to let her exercise his polo ponies every day to get herself fit for what was to come. Although she'd ridden since she was six, and although horses were by no means the only way to get around Katerina, she'd done more riding in a week than she'd done in the past year. But it had been exhilarating and more.

She'd read respect in the eyes of the Simpsons when she'd refused to complain about her aching muscles or to take to the 'bull buggy', an open four-wheel drive vehicle suitable for getting around rough terrain with fearsome bars on the front capable of repelling charging bulls.

But Joe Jordan had surprised her. There had been no more overtures of a personal nature. In fact he'd treated her exactly as he treated his sister.

Even when, without quite knowing how, they'd taken to preparing the evening meal together. He had explained solemnly to her that Sarah was not only unhandy in the kitchen but notoriously difficult when it came to getting along with household help.

'Can't tell you how many cooks she's gone through!' he'd said.

'You'd think she'd be only too happy to have someone do it for her,' Lydia had responded.

'She is, at first. But it's not easy to get good cooks prepared to bury themselves beyond the black stump, and being an extremely fastidious person, as well as a "do-gooder", it's not long before she's interfering and, worse, trying to make them over into what she believes they should be. In other words non-drinkers, non-smokers, no bad language, extremely moral, even regular churchgoers, and all the things *she* is.'

Lydia had grinned. 'I see. She's quite a character, your twin sister.'

He'd looked at her curiously. 'But you two seem to get along pretty well.'

They did, Lydia had mused. Sarah could do most things the men did, and apart from her lack of domesticity she was a born country woman—and it was obvious she loved every inch of Katerina. She was also the perfect foil for her tall, unemotional husband. 'We do. I like her very much, actually. And she hasn't, so far, tried to change me in any respect.'

'Well, you don't have any of the above vices, apart from an occasional glass of wine. That could be why.'

'It could indeed. So that's why you and I are cooking dinner together?'

'I did warn you about this.' Joe had been basting a roast chicken and Lydia preparing an apple crumble for dessert. 'And I can take her cooking for so long, but not much longer. There.' He'd closed the oven door.

'Rolf doesn't seem to mind.'

'Rolf's a man who likes peace above all else. But, contrary to Sarah's belief that she has him well and truly housetrained, et cetera, he's one of those strong, silent types, and you don't really know what is going on beneath the surface.'

'Unlike you,' Lydia had said flippantly.

'Well, I don't know about that,' he'd replied, but had made no attempt to enlarge on the issue.

Lydia thought, coming back to the present on this Sunday morning when the house was as quiet as a church, that she must have got through to him with what she'd said about Brad and Daisy. They'd certainly spent quite a bit of time together, enough for him to have made all manner of passes.

She'd spent her first couple of days learning the ropes, with either Joe or Rolf at her side.

It was hard work, mustering and drafting cattle. First of all a mob of cattle was mustered by helicopter into a yard. Then they were sorted into various categories and other yards: weaners and calves to be branded, calves to be returned to their mothers as soon as possible, or weaners old enough to be separated and educated, breeding cows and bulls that went straight back whence they came, provided they were in good condition, sale cattle—steers and bullocks—and cattle to be culled from the herd for various reasons.

At one stage each beast was put into a yard by itself for evaluation, and this was when Lydia was able to make a fast assessment on whether they needed any medical treatment. But you had to be quick, and she soon realised that most of the members of the muster team knew as much about cattle as she did.

It had been a bit sobering, but she'd pushed herself to work as hard as any other member of the team, and had thanked heaven for the polo ponies—otherwise she'd have needed a wheelchair!

But Joe and Rolf had made a point of including her in their discussions on all sorts of things including their breeding programme. Most of the stock on Katerina was now Brahman, or crossed with Brahman, but there were still some wild scrubber bulls and inbred shorthorn cows to be dealt with, and their influence eradicated from the herd.

She hadn't slept out under the stars yet—the paddocks being mustered were close to the homestead at this stage—but she'd gone to bed in her bed each night to dream of dust and grit in your teeth, hair and every fold of skin, and endless hooves, and the hot sun beating down on you until you were dizzy…

But she'd enjoyed it, she couldn't deny. And she'd enjoyed becoming known to the men who worked the mobs and being treated with growing respect.

Yet, she mused, whilst others had treated her with growing respect, including his sister, Joe Jordan had given no indication as to whether he was impressed or not.

'How like a woman!' She had to laugh as she said it out aloud, and was referring to herself. She stood up and went inside to brush her hair now it was dry, then decided to plait it in one thick plait, because it was looking quite wild with energy despite the conditioner.

And her laughter faded as she did so, because it was sobering to contemplate that she could now be slightly peeved because a man she had given the flick to, in a manner of speaking, had taken the hint.

Nor was she really peeved, she assured herself. Just a little puzzled.

Her thoughts turned to Daisy. She had spoken to Chattie the day after she'd arrived at Katerina, but her aunt had only been able to tell her that Daisy had embarked on the Musica Viva tour, which would take her away for a few weeks, and had appeared to be in good spirits. Lydia had not, for reasons she wasn't too sure of, enlightened her aunt about the principal shareholder in Katerina.

She shrugged and walked through to the kitchen, and decided to make a cake.

It was when the cake was ready to go into the oven that Joe came in and slung his hat accurately on to a hook in the hall.

'Morning, Ms Kelso. What a picture of domesticity you present!'

'Thank you! Where is everyone?'

He didn't reply.

Lydia closed the oven door, hung the oven mitt on the handle and turned to him, to find him leaning back against a counter with his arms folded and his eyes on her legs.

She went still, and he took his time about raising his gaze to hers. Then they simply stared into each other's eyes for a long moment. But Lydia discovered her mouth had gone dry and her heart was beating strangely. It was the first time Joe Jordan had seen her legs out of trousers...

He broke the moment. She'd found herself curiously mesmerised. He turned, discovered the mixing bowl on the counter, and picked up a wooden spoon to scrape some mixture out of it. 'Mmm,' he pronounced, 'ginger and good. Where is everyone? Gone to church.'

'Church...how?'

'By plane. Sarah asked me to tell you that she hadn't liked to disturb you on your first day off, and she forgot to mention last night that there was a service being held this morning on an adjoining property. They have a circuit,' he added conversationally. 'She and Rolf will also being staying on Dunoon Station for the night. They're having a bit of a get-together.'

'Oh. I see. Didn't you want to go?'

'Well, we couldn't leave you here on your own, now, could we?'

'I'd have been quite safe here on my own, I'm sure,' Lydia murmured, and moved at last. She went over to the sink and began to gather the utensils she'd been using.

He handed her the mixing bowl. 'Besides, I thought you might enjoy a swim this afternoon.'

'Where?'

'There are some water holes a few miles away. We could take a couple of horses—'

'Not horses,' she said involuntarily. 'I mean,' she added, 'I—'

'I quite understand,' he said wryly. 'I'm often as stiff as a plank after I've been away from here for a while. We could take the bull buggy.'

'Well...' Lydia hesitated.

He raised an eyebrow at her. 'That's not what you were going to say?'

'I...um...I was stiff, but it's getting better. What I was going to say—'

'I promise not to cast lecherous looks at your legs,' he murmured. 'They caught me off guard, that's all. Being a mere male and...that kind of thing.'

Lydia turned the tap on so forcefully they were both hit by a spray of droplets.

He reached over and moderated the flow. 'We could take a picnic meal and your cake. It's deliciously cool there, under the trees. There are birds to watch, brolgas and storks, and water lilies, and there's not a cow for miles, because we've fenced it off from them—we like to think it's our own little equivalent of Kakadu.'

'Kakadu? Are you joking?'

'Come and see for yourself. Meg adores the place. So you'd be responsible for denying her a favourite outing if you said no.'

'That is sheer bribery and corruption!'

'Perhaps,' he said gravely. 'But I know you and Meg like each other.'

'Oh, all right!'

* * *

'I can't believe this,' Lydia said on a breath.

Kakadu National Park, world-heritage-listed and fa-mous for its wetlands and rainforest, its Aboriginal rock art and sheer beauty, was in fact a long way from the Victoria River, Lydia knew, although still in the Northern Territory. But the idyllic spot Joe had brought her and Meg to in the bull buggy looked for all the world as if it *should* be in Kakadu.

From the vast savanna, a small creek originating from a spring had carved its way through a rocky outcrop, creating a waterfall, then a series of pools surrounded by lush vegetation. The banks were sandy, the water lilies were open in splashes of pink, white and lilac, and as they pulled up white egrets rose in slow flight to perch in the tall trees.

'Wait until you try the water,' Joe recommended. 'For anyone feeling at all stiff or sporting saddle bruising it's pure magic.'

'I don't think I can wait.' Lydia jumped out of the buggy, pulling her shorts and blouse off. She had a one-piece yellow costume on beneath, and she and Meg hit the main pool at the same time.

'Just don't tell me there are any crocodiles!' she called as she surfaced, gasping at the same time. 'I'd fight them bare-handed for this pool.'

He laughed.

'Oh, isn't this wonderful!' She dived under the water and surfaced again. 'It's so clean and cold and different from the tank water. Do you know?' She wiped her hair out of her eyes. 'I never thought I'd get rid of the dust and grit. I mean, I showered twice a day, but...' She raised her arms above her head and slid under the water again.

Joe was in when she surfaced this time. 'Sit under the waterfall,' he suggested. 'There's a ledge there.'

They swam together for the ledge and pulled themselves up as Meg barked delightedly and tried to scrabble up.

'Here you go!' Joe put his arms around the dog and lifted her bodily on to the ledge, only to almost immediately grasp his shoulder and grimace in pain.

'I thought you must be over that,' Lydia said breathlessly, as she moved her face behind the stream of water gushing down over them. 'I haven't seen any sign of it all week!'

'I'm gratified to think you were watching,' he murmured, 'but I've been very careful all week.'

'No, you haven't,' Lydia contradicted. 'Everything I've done you've done.'

'There are a lot of things I can do! It's just—it must be a certain angle, or something like that—what are you doing?'

Lydia was climbing carefully to her feet on the slippery rock. 'What I did last time. Any objections?' She knelt behind him and put her hands on his shoulder.

'I wouldn't dream of it,' he murmured.

Ten minutes later, she said, 'Well?'

'I beg your pardon?'

'Is it any better? It should have worked on a horse by now.'

He considered. 'I could be different. I could need it for longer and on an hourly basis, for example. Or do you treat all men as if they were horses so as—?'

He didn't finish for the simple reason that Lydia removed her hands from his shoulder to the middle of his back and pushed him into the pool. Unfortunately the exertion caused her to slip, and the only way she could save herself was to twist sideways and dive into the water. Meg, thinking it was all wonderful fun, jumped in almost on top of her.

But when she surfaced Joe Jordan was right beside her, and he took her into his arms.

'What do you think you're doing?' she spluttered.

'This,' he responded, and started to kiss her.

They went under, and when they came up she choked, 'More like drowning me, you idiot!'

'OK.' And he flipped her on her back and started to tow her towards the bank in a lifesaver's grip.

'I...you...' Lydia twisted and fought, then felt her feet touch the sandy bottom, and with a few more strokes they could both stand in water up to their waists.

'You're right,' he conceded, 'much easier to do it on one's feet—well, in certain circumstances.' And he started to kiss her again.

Despite his sore shoulder, Lydia discovered, he was more than a match for her. Besides, she told herself, she was breathless from all the horseplay and dunking. All the same, when he finally released her she could only stare at him wide-eyed for a long, long moment, because she had in fact stopped fighting him for other reasons...

Such as the electric feeling of fitting perfectly into his arms and the lovely shock of their wet bodies touching. The miraculous way he'd made her feel tall and slim but happy to be so, even though she was nearly as tall as he was and there had been times in her life when being five feet eleven had been a handicap. But not with Joe Jordan.

Because he'd made everything about her feel as if it had been expressly designed to please him, to feel gloriously attractive to him, and the way he'd kissed her once she'd started to feel this way had been sensationally arousing. The way he'd held her and handled her, so that she could feel his strength, but only to glory in it at the same time as she felt special and cherished. So much so that to be released had brought a pang of disappointment, and she'd only just stopped herself from reaching out to him...

'So,' he said quietly, and touched a finger to her wet cheek, 'we are in this together, Lydia, despite your assertions to the contrary.'

'I...you...' she stammered, on the brink of telling him that he could have given Casanova lessons.

He waited attentively.

She sighed. 'I knew it was too good to be true, Mr Jordan.'

CHAPTER THREE

HE DIDN'T ask her to explain immediately.

She went behind a clump of bushes and changed back into her shorts and blouse. When she reappeared he was lighting a small fire on the sand. There was a tripod over it with a blackened can hanging from it.

'Genuine billy tea,' he said conversationally as she hesitated with her towel in her hand.

'Oh.' She gave her hair a final rub dry and hung the towel on the bull bars of the buggy. Then she ran her fingers through it a couple of times and let it settle, and started to plait it again.

'Here.' He pulled a cushion forward. 'Take a pew. I thought tea and a piece of your cake first, then, when we feel hungry again, I brought a couple of steaks.'

He hadn't changed, just added a shirt over his damp shorts.

They said nothing until the billy boiled and he threw in a handful of tea leaves. Lydia got the ginger cake out of the esky, discovered some butter and buttered some slices, one of which she gave to Meg. Joe poured the tea into thick china mugs.

'This cake is delicious,' he pronounced. 'Did he teach you to cook?'

'Brad? No, my aunt Chattie was mostly responsible, but I think one really teaches oneself to cook, don't you? Either you have the interest or you don't.'

'True,' he conceded, 'although in my case it was a survival technique too. My mother was just like Sarah, so we grew up with a series of disastrous cooks—you learnt to fend for yourself.'

Lydia looked at him, slightly interested. 'Did your parents carve Katerina out of the wilderness, so to speak?'

'They did. They came here as a young couple very much in love. They survived drought, flood, pestilence, and gradually built up a herd. It was all the more remarkable because my mother was an English schoolteacher, born in the country and mad about horses, but there's a big difference.'

'What about your father?'

'He grew up in outback Queensland. He was from a grazing family.'

'Why don't you...' Lydia paused '...carry on the tradition?'

Joe stretched out on the sand and leant on his elbow, his good side. 'I was always torn between Katerina and the big smoke. So when Rolf arrived on the scene, proved his worth and—later, of course—married Sarah, it seemed like an opportunity to go out and try to make my name in another field. In this game you're always hostage to so many imponderables: weather, beef prices and so on. It's not a bad idea to have a couple of strings to your bow. But part of me will always live here.'

'Did you expect to succeed as well as you did?'

He was silent.

Lydia smiled. 'You did.'

He shrugged a shade ruefully. 'Perhaps, but not in the field I have succeeded in.'

'Tell me,' she invited.

'I majored in political science and English at university. I intended to become a journalist, a serious journalist. It was quite by accident that a bit of a talent for sketching saw me go down another road—although it is a form of journalism.'

'So you don't...' she paused '...paint or sketch or draw for any other reason?'

'No. I'm good at drawing funny faces to go with pithy captions; that's about it.'

'You, as well as Sarah and Rolf, need some strong sons to help you carry on the tradition here,' Lydia commented.

Joe hesitated. 'It's probably Sarah's place to tell you this, but she's had a few problems in that area. That's why they're taking this break. It's not exactly a holiday; they're joining an *in vitro* fertilisation programme.'

Lydia blinked and sipped her tea. 'I hope they're successful.'

He sat up. 'Otherwise it will be left to me to provide heirs. Just think what Daisy could have robbed Katerina of.'

Lydia glanced heavenwards.

'Have you heard how she is?' he asked.

'Away on a Musica Viva tour. No, I haven't been able to catch up with her personally.'

'Then should we discuss how Daisy didn't appear to even cross your mind not that long ago?' He gestured towards the pool.

'Let's not,' Lydia murmured.

'OK.' He looked quite obliging. 'I'm all for banning Daisy from looming up between us, but you said you knew it was too good to be true. What did you mean?'

'I...spoke without thinking.'

'Lydia,' he murmured, 'did you also kiss me without thinking?'

The sun was starting to set and the shadows of the trees were lengthening across the series of pools. Since they'd come out of the water the birds had gradually returned from the trees and were stalking through the shallows. The sound of the waterfall was oddly soothing.

'I've never,' she said slowly, 'been kissed against my will before. So I didn't really think. I...got carried along, I guess. That's all.'

He was silent again, and much as she would have wished otherwise she couldn't resist the flow of something between them that forced her to look into his eyes at last. And she had to flinch inwardly at the scepticism she saw in their hazel depths.

'All right,' she said abruptly. 'When I said I knew it was too good to be true I meant that I'd found it hard to believe you had given up all aspirations towards me. Men—'

'That was Plan B,' he broke in. 'But go on. Men...?'

'Can be extremely annoying,' she said through her teeth. 'But the most annoying thing of all, if you must know, was to find that I was even thinking about it. Although before you get your hopes up, Mr Jordan, most *women* suffer from—well, we're just human, I guess, and I couldn't help wondering why, or how, you could switch off me just like that!'

He raised an eyebrow. 'That's rather honest.'

'It doesn't mean to say I still wouldn't have given you the flick,' she answered with irony.

'So you don't mind being desired—?'

'It means,' she pressed on, disregarding, 'one would prefer to think one was desirable as opposed to as forgettable as an old shoe. End of story.'

'I see.'

She could see he was trying not to laugh, and she made a disgusted sound but was annoyed to find herself feeling hot all over. Possibly the result of making a fool of herself and *not* being entirely honest.

'I think I'd better tell you about Plan B,' he said gravely. 'When you explained about your husband, as well as your sister—who is not in love with me, by the way, but let's not digress—I realised that I'd been clumsy and heavy-handed and it might be a good idea for us to get to know each other better before I made any more—moves.'

Lydia's dark blue eyes widened.

'However, your legs bowled me over,' he said apologetically. 'Then, to see you frolicking like a mermaid, so naturally and joyfully, compounded things. But what really brought the worst out in me was being treated like a horse and—manhandled again.'

'I—didn't.'

He smiled wryly. 'Well, you are a vet, and you have a singular knack of making me feel like a piece of horse-flesh when you're manipulating my shoulder, and you can't deny you've pushed me around a couple of times.'

'So that was revenge?' Lydia said incredulously.

'Not exactly. It was more like beating my manly chest to warn you that you may have taken me by surprise a couple of times but not to depend on getting away with it for ever.'

He said it quite seriously, but Lydia knew he was laughing at her, and to her amazement she found herself smiling reluctantly, then actually laughing at herself.

'I feel like an Amazon,' she said ruefully, at last.

'Don't,' he advised. 'You are talking to a slightly wounded ego, I have to confess. But...' He paused, and all of a sudden she sensed that he was completely sober as he went on, 'Proving that I *could* kiss you, whether you were willing or not, is not quite the same thing as wanting to kiss you.'

She swallowed.

'Or you enjoying being kissed by me,' he added.

She looked down at her hands, still clasping her mug, and put it down carefully. 'How not to feel a fool,' she murmured. 'Yes, I enjoyed it, but then I think I always knew I'd enjoy being kissed by you.'

She saw the flicker of surprise in his eyes.

'Put it this way,' she went on with a little shrug, and flicked her plait back. 'I didn't think it was that easy to define when we first met, but—I guess you exude a certain amount, if not to say rather a lot, of sex appeal, Joe. And I could suddenly see what Daisy obviously saw in you. As well as many others, no doubt.'

'Crikey,' he murmured, and stood up.

'Most men would be delighted to hear that.'

'I'm not most men,' he said witheringly. 'If I'd said something similar to you—'

'What's so different about you telling me you had this curious desire to see me without my clothes?' she countered, stung. 'If we're discussing being made to feel like an object!'

'Rubbish,' he retorted. 'All I'm trying to do is admit that we've had a "curious" effect on each other from the moment we laid eyes on one another.'

'And all I'm trying to do is point out why. But I'll put it plainer, if you like,' Lydia said dangerously. 'As I said at the time, your reputation preceded you, Mr Jordan. On top of which, Daisy thought enough of you to want you for the father of her child—who would *not* have wondered about you? But what you really thought of me was encapsulated in your cartoon.' She stopped abruptly and eyed him narrowly. 'You wouldn't have had a bet with yourself, by any chance?'

His sudden stillness gave him away.

Lydia made a disgusted sound and stood up to walk over to the edge of the pool.

He didn't follow suit, but watched her thoughtfully as she stared into the water with her arms folded. With that long-legged, coltish grace and her hair in a plait she looked about sixteen, he thought. But she hadn't kissed him like a novice teenager and one couldn't doubt she had a sharp brain and a mature outlook. He said quietly, 'Was that a stab in the dark?'

She looked over her shoulder at him. 'It obviously hit home.'

'OK. I did have a bet with myself.' He shrugged. 'But if we're talking about honest reactions, that's the way men tend to think, and is it any different from enjoying being desired rather than discarded like an old shoe—by *anyone*?'

'What was the bet?' Lydia enquired in arctic tones.

'That you would like to come to bed with me one day.'

She swung around and gazed at him fiercely. 'Take me home, Joe Jordan!'

'Not before we've sorted something else out, Lydia Kelso,' he drawled. 'Could you be so worked up because you've found you're coming out of the shell of grief and missing your Brad and don't know how to handle it?'

'With a man who talks about making "moves" on me, has bets with himself about me and has bedded my sister? You couldn't be more right!'

'I—'

'Just take me home.' Her shoulders slumped. 'I don't want to talk about it any more.' She shivered suddenly.

'Here.' He pulled a jacket out of the buggy and handed it to her.

She accepted it reluctantly. It was his jacket, a khaki battle jacket, and she draped it over her shoulders, then went to sit in the buggy.

'Lydia,' he murmured, 'you're wasting your time.'

'What do you mean?'

He was unpacking the esky, which she suddenly saw contained a lot more than she'd realised. He straightened and gazed at her. And her nerves tightened unexpectedly. She recognised an easy finality about him, and not only that, a very adult masculinity, and he was, damn him, the only man who had intrigued her since Brad.

He said, 'We're not going home. In fact we're going to spend the night here. I tossed a couple of swags into the back.' He gestured at the buggy. 'We're going to cook steak and sausages, have a singsong and tell stories around the fire. We won't discuss anything you don't want to discuss and you don't have to worry that I'll take advantage of your person. That's what we'll be doing.'

'You can't! You can't just...do this!'

His lips twisted and he patted his pocket. 'I can. I happen to be in possession of the keys.'

'But I might not have wanted to do this ever before...before...' she stammered.

'Before we fell out? I think there are a few things you *think* you might not want to do, Lydia, but this one I'm sure you'll enjoy. Look, I'm not going to touch you, so you can sulk there, if you wish, or you could help me cook these steaks.' He bent down to continue unpacking the esky.

As the sun cast its first rays over the horizon the next morning, Lydia sat up and looked around dazedly. Then she went still, because there was a kangaroo drinking at one of the pools and some strange, tall birds she couldn't identify in another. She put her hand on Meg's collar and they watched and listened to the dawn and its chorus in sheer wonder—at least on Lydia's part.

She turned her head at last to see that Joe was awake and watching her. 'Brolgas?' she mouthed.

He nodded.

An hour later she was drinking hot coffee and eating a heated-up sausage in a roll. Despite having slept on the sand in a swag, she was not stiff. Joe had scraped out hollows for them, but she'd also had another swim. The water had been freezing, but marvellously refreshing, and she felt, she reflected, as good as she'd ever felt in her life.

She cupped her mug and glanced sideways at Joe Jordan. For she was wondering how to thank a man who had basically kidnapped her, for such a night to remember.

He hadn't laid a finger on her, but after they'd eaten their steaks, washed down with some red wine, he'd brought out a battered old mouth organ, and, soothed by food and wine, who would *not* have put aside their slightly chilly demeanour and relaxed beneath the stars with the fire built up to some bush ballads? Even joined in with her rather husky contralto?

She blinked suddenly as she realised he was looking back at her, and said, 'I know what you meant.'

He raised an eyebrow at her.

'About not taking advantage of my *person*. It was my soul you...' She stopped and looked away.

'Stole?' he suggested.

'Not quite, but soothed. Thanks. You were right; it was great.'

Joe ran his fingers over the shadows on his jaw, then through his hair, causing it to stand up in peaks. She was wearing his jacket again, but he didn't seem to feel the cold, nor did he have the look about him this morning of a man who would plot and plan to hold someone against her will. He looked disarmingly relaxed, even boyishly charming, bare-legged in the same shorts and shirt of the day before, which was to say that he looked quite harmless.

Then he stood up and stretched, and his physique caused Lydia's heartbeat to alter subtly. His legs were long, his waist and hips lean, his shoulders wide and powerful. And it occurred to her that all she'd seen him do over the past week—as good as any man on the property but more than that, with a particular ease and grace that made him a pleasure to watch on a horse—must have represented quite some will-power and toughness if his shoulder was still hurting him.

So he was something of an enigma, Joe Jordan, she was musing, when she realised he'd said her name. And realised her eyes were still on him, and that another plane of her mind was still registering all the things, all the physical things about him, that appealed to her.

She swallowed, and admonished herself for allowing herself to be affected in any way by the physical aspect of this man. And managed to say calmly, 'Yes?'

'I think it might be an idea to pack up and go. It's still early and we can beat the Simpsons home.'

She got up with sudden alacrity as a vision of his sister Sarah's curiosity at what might have transpired here in this delightful place overnight took hold of her.

'I couldn't agree more—and if no one asks I don't intend to tell them we spent the night here.'

He grinned, but said, 'It's what I had in mind as well. The protection of your fair reputation, Ms Kelso, although—'

'I know, I know.' She waved a hand. 'But people tend to imagine all sorts of things, so let's get this show on the road.'

They did. They were all loaded, Lydia was seated beside him in the front, Meg was perched in the back with her tongue lolling out happily, but when he put the key in and turned it, nothing happened.

Half an acrimonious hour later, they'd worked out the problem. On the journey from the homestead they must have hit a rock that had caused a fuel line to spring a fine leak, thereby gradually draining the tank along the way, and they must have coasted into the clearing around the pools and waterfall on the last drops of fuel in the tank.

'I don't believe this!'

'You've said that before,' Joe responded. 'By the way, where did you learn about mechanics?'

'What does it *matter*,' she replied impatiently. 'How could you not have noticed what was happening from the fuel gauge?'

'The fuel gauge hasn't been working for the last couple of days. That's why I filled it up.'

She stared at him frustratedly.

'Lydia, it's just one of those things,' he said serenely. 'And you've got grease on your chin. We'll be found, believe me.'

'The object of the exercise was not to be found! Now, not only will people be wondering all sorts of things but we'll be the laughing stock of the place—what are you doing?' she demanded as he took the esky out.

'I'm going to make you a cup of tea just now. There's more ginger cake.'

'I don't suppose you thought to bring more fuel,' she said witheringly.

'Assuming I had, which I didn't, to make space for the swags, we'd still have the problem—unless you're that good you can fix a fuel line in the middle of the bush? Were you proposing to wrap it up in your hanky?'

'Oh!' she groaned, in the most heartfelt way. 'Why are men so superior?'

'Now, Lydia,' he recommended, 'perhaps we shouldn't get on to that topic, because it could lead to other things about men. For example, we're hot, bothered and dirty, so I intend to have a swim—so should you, incidentally—and then I could recommend the perfect way to…ease your frustration. Were you to allow yourself to be thoroughly kissed, you'd find yourself feeling much better.'

Her mouth dropped open and stayed open for a moment, until she said feebly, 'How old do you think I am, Joe Jordan?'

'I know how old you are; you told me yourself—twenty-six, going on sixty.'

'I didn't say that,' she protested, and stopped.

'You didn't have to.'

Lydia put her hands on her hips and tossed her hair. 'What are you implying now?'

'Nothing.' He shrugged and pulled his shirt off. 'But come in,' he invited. 'At least this part of the cure comes with no strings attached.' And he waded into the water.

'How do I know you're not going to beat your manly chest again?'

'You don't.' He sank beneath the surface and came up with his hair plastered to his head, then started to wade towards her. 'Are you coming in or not?' he asked dangerously.

'Stay there,' she commanded, but not quite as forcefully as she would have wished. 'I...I've got to change first.'

They were drinking their tea when the Bell 45 flew overhead, then came back to hover over the clearing. Pete leant out and gave them the thumbs-up, but there was not enough clear space to land. Joe gestured to the bull buggy and gave the thumbs-down sign. Pete waved and flew off.

'See?' Joe said to Lydia. 'Help will be with us shortly. He'll radio through to the homestead.'

'Help in the form of horses?' she enquired.

'No, a truck that we can load the buggy on to, with a tow line and a winch.'

She sipped her tea. 'I didn't really believe you'd do it.'

'Do it?' He raised an eyebrow at her, causing her to bite her lip with annoyance, because Joe Jordan had not laid a finger on her, yet again, and, worse, found her obvious wariness amusing.

'Kiss me,' she elucidated gloomily.

'Is that an invitation?'

'No.'

'You weren't about to take the risk, however?' he hazarded.

She shrugged.

'Never mind,' he said comfortingly. 'I don't think any the less of you.'

Lydia frowned. 'What do you mean?'

'That I don't think it was wimpish of you to decide discretion might be better than valour in the circumstances but rather wise, that's all. If that's what was worrying you.'

She stared at him with her lips compressed, as much with annoyance towards herself as him. Because he'd spelt out her vague feeling of dissatisfaction with herself and, in doing so, had made her feel ridiculous. 'You are too clever by half, Joe Jordan,' she said bitterly.

'It's how I make a living,' he replied flippantly. 'But you're not half bad yourself. Where did you learn to strip an engine like that?'

She breathed deeply and took hold. If there was a way to counter the unsettling effect this man was having on her, it certainly wasn't the way she was going about it. 'The boy next door,' she said wryly.

He laughed. 'A boyfriend?'

'No. We grew up together because we were neighbours and the same age, and he was mad about motors. I used to help him. Eventually we progressed from lawn mowers to cars, although along the way we designed and produced a motorised go-cart.' She grinned. 'When we nearly killed ourselves in it, we were banned from using it.'

'How did you nearly kill yourselves?' he asked, looking genuinely entertained.

'Well, the brakes failed as we were tearing down the drive, a long, sloping drive, and he ended up in the gutter and I came to rest in the hedge. He broke his arm. I just suffered cuts and bruises. His mother was particularly mad with me. I can remember her yelling—"Boys are bad enough, Lydia, you expect them to do crazy things, but girls should know better..." She got an awful fright.'

'So,' he said slowly, but with an assessing glint in his eye, 'a bit of a tomboy?'

She shrugged. 'I baked her this wonderful cake to say sorry for all the trauma we'd caused her. But, yes, I was always more interested in how things worked and, of course, animals rather than clothes, et cetera. That came later.'

'I think I'd like to have known you when you were growing up,' he said thoughtfully.

'What were you like?'

He raised his eyebrows and stroked Meg's head. 'A bit of a handful, I see now in hindsight. I didn't get on that well with my father. Possibly because while Sarah has never had any ambition to be anywhere else but Katerina, I did.'

'I'm sorry,' Lydia said sincerely.

He glanced at her narrowly, as if seeking an explanation for her sincerity.

'It's just, well, I've often wondered how my mother, who was a lot like Daisy, apparently, would have coped with a changeling like me.'

'You don't really see yourself as a changeling, do you?'

'No, not exactly. What I meant was, I'm different, and I think that can be hard for one's same-sex parent to cope with, but especially, perhaps, for fathers, who want to be able to pass on what they've carved out to their sons.'

'That's rather like—hitting the nail on the head,' he said ruefully, then paused with his head raised.

Lydia heard it a moment later: the sound of a truck.

He looked back at her. 'Rescue, salvation, whatever you like to call it, is at hand, Lydia.'

She swallowed, but couldn't tear her gaze away, and

she felt her skin prickle because of an awareness of this man on several levels, now. Not only the physical, but an inkling of the currents that flowed beneath the surface and had helped shape him into something of an enigma. A feeling that there was more depth to Joe Jordan than some of his attitudes implied, as well as the uncertainty he provoked in her—he might not have touched her against her will after that first kiss, but she wasn't sure she could always rely on it.

They were still staring into each other's eyes when the truck laboured down the causeway, with Rolf at the wheel.

When they got back to the homestead, Sarah, as it happened, was not immediately curious about her brother and Lydia's night out under the stars. True, there was a slightly narrow look cast in Lydia's direction but that was the extent of it. The reason for this abstention might have been the result of Sarah finding herself on the receiving end of a pointed look of his own from Joe. Or it might have been because she'd come home from Dunoon full of plans to organise a 'B&S' ball the following Saturday night.

'A ball!' Joe said exasperatedly. 'We're in the middle of the mustering season, Sarah! And it gives you less than a week.'

'I don't need a week. And it can be our farewell party before we go away. It'll also give Lydia a chance to meet some of our neighbours.'

'Are we talking about a Bachelor and Spinster Ball?' Lydia asked.

'A synonym for any excuse to have a bash,' Joe said cynically. 'More than fifty per cent of the invitees will be married.'

'Who cares?' Sarah said blithely. 'Joe, be a darling and get in touch with Lefty Murdoch and his mates, for the music. Rolf is going to clean up the small shed—aren't you, my sweet? And I've arranged for the Dunoon cook to handle the food. We've just got to provide barbecues and spits—and, of course, the meat.'

'Thank heavens for one small mercy,' Joe intoned.

Causing his sister to say, 'You're not in a very good mood, beloved. Why don't you go and create a cartoon?'

He went, muttering beneath his breath.

That was when Sarah chose to voice her thoughts about the night Lydia and Joe had spent together. 'Keep knocking him back, Lydia. It's about time some woman did,' she said, with a conspiratorial smile, and she waltzed off leaving Lydia blinking dazedly.

'I didn't bring anything to wear to a ball, Sarah,' Lydia said several days later.

Sarah laughed. 'Well, we do try to be innovative and dressy, and most of the men wear dinner jackets even if it's with jeans, but let me take a look at what you did bring and I'll pass judgement.'

'My dear Lydia,' she said a few minutes later, holding up the only dress Lydia had brought—and then only because she'd been quite sure Brad's parents would take her out to dinner in Townsville. 'What do you mean you don't have a dress?'

'But it's short. It's not really a ball thing; it's—'

'Divine,' Sarah said of the simple black silk georgette dress studded with silver metal embroidery. She looked at the label. 'Ah. No wonder! No, its beauty will lie in the fact that it's not a ball dress, but I can just picture you looking stunning in it—stunning enough to sock Joe right between the eyes.'

Lydia sat down on her bed. 'Sarah, Joe has not addressed two words to me for the last few days.'

'I know, he's been going around like a bear with a sore head, but that generally is because he's either been thwarted or he's finding it hard to get inspiration.'

'Daisy said he could be moody...' Lydia realised she'd spoken without thinking.

Sarah raised an eyebrow. 'Your sister?'

'The same.'

'Well, she's right. But if you just ignore it, it doesn't last. Look, I've got to dash. Rolf is complaining mightily about all the time he's spending on the shed, so I said I'd give him a hand. Would you be sweet enough to do dinner for me tonight?'

'Of course,' Lydia murmured, and stood up to hang up her dress.

She was having an easy day because the men, most of them, were setting up portable yards in a new paddock for the next muster. In fact the next two days until the ball were going to be easy for her—one of the huge road trains used to transport the mustered stock had broken down and would be delayed, so the muster itself would be delayed.

Not that she'd sat around doing nothing. She'd also helped with the shed, helped a mare with a difficult foaling, and spent some time on the team that was educating the weaners so that in future musters they would be easy to handle and know what was required of them before they were returned to the herd.

She went to the kitchen and started dinner. When the roast lamb was in the oven, the potatoes and pumpkin peeled and the green vegetables prepared, she poured herself a glass of wine and went to sit on the back step to watch the sunset. Meg immediately joined her, indicating that Joe must be home, although she hadn't heard him come in. It caused her to smile faintly to think that he could be avoiding her.

Was this Plan C? she wondered.

But almost as soon as she'd wondered it he wandered out onto the verandah—with a beer in his hand, and there was an air about him that she instantly recognised, a relaxed air.

'So it *was* a lack of inspiration rather than—' she said, and stopped ruefully.

He sat down on the step beside her. 'If you're referring to my uncommunicative attitude for the past few days, yes, but how the hell could you tell and how can you now tell it's over?'

'My father,' she explained. 'He goes through the same thing. Mind you, I wouldn't call it uncommunicative, downright moody is a better description—but when he's over it he has this rather beatific, relaxed air about him. That's exactly how you look at the moment.'

He raised an eyebrow. 'I apologise for being so transparent, but what was your second scenario?'

Lydia bit her lip, because she'd been hoping he would ignore what she'd left unsaid. Faint hope with this man, she mused. 'Just something your sister said,' she murmured.

'Don't tell me,' he drawled. 'Sarah is even more transparent than I am. She thinks I'm in a mood because I'm not getting my way with you, no doubt.'

'Just goes to show how wrong you can be, even a sister,' Lydia remarked, not without some complacency.

'She's not wrong at all.'

The sun had set, but its rays were still illuminating the sky with streaks of orange, and a living, fleeting rose-pink that almost made you want to catch your breath it was so beautiful was colouring the dusty countryside beyond the garden fence.

Lydia watched it fade before she turned her head to Joe Jordan. 'I don't know what to say.'

'Obviously.'

'So did it have anything at all to do with not being able to create?'

'Sure.' He shrugged. 'A double whammy for me again—I really don't know what I've done to deserve it,' he added plaintively.

'Well, tell me about the other one,' she said a little helplessly.

He looked at her with some irony before saying, 'OK. I am in fact on official leave at the moment. Someone else has taken over from me. But in the event of Sarah and Rolf having to spend more time down south, which is a possibility, then I'm going to have to spend more time up here. So I thought I'd have a go at doing things at long distance, so to speak. It's almost impossible.'

'But you said technology, et cetera, made it possible to pursue your career up here.'

'I was hoping it would. But I need to be right there, with my finger on the pulse.'

'I see.' Lydia blinked at the growing dusk. 'You couldn't get in another manager?'

'It's not easy, and I want Sarah and Rolf to be able to relax and give this shot at having a baby a real go without having to worry about Katerina. They deserve it.'

'So,' she said slowly, 'what were you looking so relaxed and beatific about?'

He grinned. 'Well, it wasn't some devilish plan to have my way with you, Lydia. No, I've made a decision. I'm taking the next nine months off.'

'Will—*can you*, without prejudicing your future?'

'Time will tell. In the meantime I'm going to transfer my creative skills to something a bit different. A weekly column about the outback.'

'That's very...very decent of you,' Lydia said.

'Ah, but it is only you, dear Lydia, who has doubts about my decency,' he countered, and raised his beer can.

Lydia glanced sideways and saw the smooth muscles of his tanned throat work as he swallowed some beer. For some reason it caused her to shiver noticeably, and when he asked if she was cold, and she said she was, she was miserably aware that she was telling a lie. Worse, she was also aware that she might not have deceived him, judging from the glint of something in his eyes that was at the same time amused and faintly sardonic.

But he made no move to stop her when she got up and went inside to tend to dinner. Nor did he offer to help.

She tossed and turned in bed for a while that night before she could get to sleep as she examined her feelings about Joe Jordan. Especially in light of what he'd done for Sarah and Rolf. And not only that, he was right, she mused. There was an undoubted attraction about him for her, and she was forced to face the fact that she could be coming out of her shell of grief and loneliness for Brad, and didn't know how to handle it.

But a physical attraction was one thing, she reflected. Being soul-partners with a man was another. Having once had it, she could never settle for less... And, of course, pertaining to the point was—what was he look-

ing for? Just the settlement of a bet he'd had with himself?

She flinched as she thought of it and reflected that
there was a lot to be wary about regarding Joe. Then she
sighed and reminded herself there was more than that.
There was Daisy.

Two nights later she dressed for the ball.

The shed, open on two sides and strung with gas
lights, streamers and kerosene lanterns, no longer resem-
bled a rather rusty iron structure with a concrete floor.
Square bales of hay had been set about and draped with
colourful covers. Trestle tables had been erected and
Sarah had produced a wide variety of cloths to cover
them. Green boughs tied with ribbon had been hung up,
and several barbecues and open fires just outside the
shed were glowing in the darkness.

All afternoon a steady stream of light planes and four-
wheel drives had been converging on Katerina, and the
trestle tables were starting to groan beneath an array of
food. Joe and Rolf had already started the spit roasting
of the meat, but the Dunoon chef had arrived now and
taken over.

Lydia had been down with Sarah to put the last
touches to things. Whilst some people were staying over
at the homestead, a lot were camping under the wings
of their planes, or in tents beside their vehicles. Lydia
had looked around in some amazement, because it was
as if a small community had grown up around the small
shed—a misnomer, actually. It was a large shed, just
smaller than the others.

And she'd complimented Sarah on achieving all this
in less than a week as they'd walked back to the house.

'Oh, we're all old hands at this. Not that we do it that

often. But you have to make your own entertainment up here. I'm feeling very happy,' Sarah had confided. 'Joe told me he'd mentioned to you why Rolf and I are going away?'

'He did.' Lydia had taken Sarah's hand and squeezed it gently. 'I hope and pray it will be successful for you.'

'You're sweet, Lydia. And I can't help feeling—I know it sounds stupid—but with this kind of a send-off, we might be. It's also such a load off our minds to know that Joe is happy to stay and look after things, should we need to be away for longer. They did advise me I'd be better off closer to civilisation.'

All the same, Lydia reflected as she dressed, she was curiously reluctant to go to this ball.

No, not curiously reluctant, she amended. She knew exactly the cause of her reluctance. It had a name. Joe...

CHAPTER FOUR

HE WAS the first person she bumped into as she stepped out on to the verandah from her room. He was doing the same.

And because the homestead was lit up like a Christmas tree, they could see each other with extraordinary clarity.

Lydia had started to say something, although she had no idea what it was, but she closed her mouth and found herself unable to do anything but accept his scrutiny.

The black silk georgette was simply styled, a vee-neck, cap sleeved, waistless panelled style that hugged her figure to the hips then flared slightly about her knees. The silver metallic embroidery was dotted over the material like tiny bursts of starlight and swirled into a denser cluster down one flank. With it she wore a pair of elegant, closed-toe sandals with small heels.

It was a dress that showed off her legs to advantage and her figure in a way that brought it into its own—her long, slender waist and unexpectedly feminine hips.

She'd also put her hair up in a smooth pleat and stroked some mascara on to her lashes. She wore a silver bangle in place of her watch, and Brad's signet ring, which she'd had made smaller, on her little finger, as always.

Joe Jordan looked up into her eyes at last and murmured, 'You should have warned me.'

'I...what do you mean?'

'When I saw you in your togs it occurred to me that I could dress you far better than you dressed yourself—'

'Now don't start, Joe,' she broke in wearily.

'No, I mean...' he looked rueful '...choose a style of clothes for you to wear that would make you look stunning rather than hiding your figure in mannish suits.'

She breathed exasperatedly. 'That was the only time you've seen me out of work clothes or shorts!'

'All the same, I wasn't to know you could dress like this. My apologies—unless this dress was an accidental choice?' he said gravely.

'You're...you are impossible!' she accused.

'Perhaps. But why *do* you hide behind those suits?'

'Hide what?' She stopped and tried to recover her composure. 'That I'm a bit of a beanpole?' she asked with amusement. 'And not fashioned in the least like my sister Daisy?' The last bit slipped out less amusedly.

He put his head on one side and allowed his hazel gaze to travel up and down her figure again. 'No, you're not, but in fact you could be classier than D—' He stopped as her hand flashed out and struck his cheek.

'Don't you dare insult my sister,' she breathed at the same time, then stopped, both shocked and amazed at what she'd done. Her lips parted. 'I...'

But she couldn't go on, and Joe Jordan touched his cheek then took the hand she'd used in a hard grip. 'I think I'll keep this weapon in my possession while I say what I'm going to say. I was only talking about a certain elegance you display that is less obvious than your sister Daisy's charms, therefore all the more surprising, and, yes, classier, to my mind.'

Lydia tried to pull free but he wouldn't let her.

'I haven't finished, Lydia,' he murmured dryly. 'And

if your beloved Brad didn't make you aware of this, then he may not have been the man you took him for.'

She gasped, coloured brilliantly, and her eyes darkened to midnight-blue. 'Oh, yes, he was, Joe Jordan. He used to tell me he adored my hips and legs and every beanpole inch of me. He made me feel wonderful in his arms and what was more, he gave me the courage to dress for comfort when I wanted to and not give a damn about what other men thought,' she said proudly. 'Will you let me go?'

He released her hand abruptly and she turned on her heel and left him standing where he was.

Meg wandered up to her master, and after a moment he bent down and patted her head. At the same time he said, 'What is it about her that brings out all the worst in me, Meg?'

Predictably, Meg didn't answer.

Why, why, why?

It was something Lydia asked herself over and over during the rest of what turned out to be a very long evening. Why had she allowed herself to be taunted into making personal statements of such a nature? Why had she resorted to slapping his face when she'd never done anything like that in her entire life? But who wouldn't take offence at being told they didn't know how to dress, that their sister was not classy and that their beloved husband might not have been much of a man?

Not to mention the mere fact that *he* was a man who *could* comment on her sister's figure, she thought bitterly at one point.

Throughout this internal dialogue with herself she was introduced to a lot of people. She danced to Lefty Murdoch's band, she talked, laughed and ate, and at one point got quite cross with herself for not being able to give this unique experience her all. Her being furious just below the surface would always colour this version of a Bachelor and Spinster Ball, way up in the VRD of the Northern Territory, where a lot of the men *did* wear evening jackets with jeans and boots and tall, wide cowboy hats and where part of the food was a roast pig on a spit.

Some of the gowns were magnificently formal—despite the fact that their wearers had dressed in a tent or under the wing of a plane—and her own dress came in for plenty of compliments on its sheer, simple elegance. And Joe Jordan was obviously delighting his neighbours with his presence, although he hadn't followed the dinner jacket and jeans fashion, but wore a blue long-sleeved shirt with button-down pockets, a dark red tie and bone-coloured moleskins.

She sat down on a bale of straw at one point and fanned herself with her hand, then discovered Meg beside her. 'It's not fair,' she said to the dog. 'You're so gorgeous and your master is a complete pig!'

Meg lifted her paw gravely. Lydia shook it, smiling reluctantly and saying, 'Oh, well, I don't suppose you can agree with me—what's that you've got on your collar?'

It turned out to be a note tied to the dog's collar with a piece of string. What was more, it had her name on it. She untied it with a frown and opened it. It was a cartoon. A Joe Jordan look-alike was banging his head against a wall in despair. A Lydia Kelso look-alike, even to the dress she was wearing at that moment, was walking away from him. The caption was 'HOW CAN I SAY I'M SORRY? I AM, TRULY.'

She gazed at it, then, as a shadow fell across her,

gazed up at the author and moistened her lips. 'How did you know Meg would get it to me?'

'I have unlimited faith in Meg. She even forgives me when she shouldn't. When I've been a complete pig.'

Prepared to see amusement lurking in those hazel eyes, Lydia was amazed to find none.

'May I find you something to drink and somewhere a bit quieter to drink it?' he queried.

She hesitated.

'Lydia,' he said quietly, 'there seems to be some confusion between us on one point at least. I never slept with Daisy; I never even gave her cause to think I would.'

'Why didn't you tell me this straight away?'

They were back up at the homestead on their own, having found no quiet spot around the shed. When he'd looked at her with a question in his eyes she'd agreed that she'd had enough of the B&S ball.

And once again they were sitting in the garden, with the sounds of revelry carried to them faintly through the chilly night air. Lydia had gone to her room and put on a long silver cashmere cardigan. Joe had made them coffee laced with whisky to counteract the chill, especially after the frenzy of the ball. The homestead was still lit up like a Christmas tree.

To say that she was still feeling dazed was true. Because she hadn't known what to say until this moment.

'Why didn't Daisy tell you?' he murmured.

She shrugged. 'Daisy has a habit of clamming up about things like that. But I was pretty sure. That still doesn't explain why *you* didn't, on one of the several opportunities you had to tell me yourself.'

He crossed his hands behind his head and gazed up at the stars. 'I think,' he said slowly, 'I was waiting for the right opportunity to give it the most impact. Mind you, I did start to tell you a couple of times, but on the last occasion at least, you cut me off.'

She started to speak several times then, said, 'Would you explain what you mean by "the most impact"?'

'Before I do that...' He frowned. 'I was not to know what Daisy *had* told you.'

'I took it as read, I'm afraid,' Lydia said. 'I...I...well, Daisy's walking around listening to her biological clock ticking. She seems quite obsessed with it and she did say a couple of things that—well—led me to think—and then there was your reputation.' She stopped a little help-lessly.

He grimaced, but made no comment.

'You are fairly renowned for escorting beautiful women around the place,' she pointed out.

'If you're asking me whether I sleep with them all, no, I don't, although I can't deny there have been a few relationships down the years. So, no, I don't sleep around on a casual basis, Lydia. I do possess a few scru-ples, not to mention a sense of self-preservation, and that's why I didn't fall in with Daisy's suggestion.'

He paused, then went on, 'As a matter of fact, I like Daisy. She's fun and I think she'd be a good friend.'

'But you must have had some idea that she was want-ing to be more than a friend,' Lydia objected.

Joe Jordan sighed and looked up at the starry heavens with, to Lydia's surprise, a distinct air of remorse. 'I may not have given it a lot of thought.'

She made a slight sound.

'I know,' he went on. 'I can be like that at the best of times, and this was not one of them.' He looked down

and across at her. 'I had this situation looming.' He gestured to encompass Katerina, and Rolf and Sarah.

Poor Daisy, crossed Lydia's mind. She said, with
some irony, although Joe was not to know it was mostly
self-directed, 'Tell me about this "most impact" bit,
then?'

He frowned. 'It's a little hard to define—'

'You wouldn't have been waiting to use it when it
was about the only thing left that would redeem you?'
she asked with some cynicism.

He said soberly, 'I asked Meg what it was about you
that brought out the worst in me…I'm sorry, it was un-
forgivable. But, no, I don't think it was that, although
that's undoubtedly how I used it. I guess I was hoping
to use it to remove the last traces of doubt you may have
had about what we do to each other.'

Lydia was struck silent.

'All the same,' he added 'when you're unfairly
painted the deepest black, you tend to be defiant—that
is, if you're me.'

Lydia couldn't help the shadow of a smile touching
her lips. 'I believe you,' she murmured, and sipped her
coffee.

He sat up. 'So, having removed Daisy for once and
for all, where do we stand now?'

'I…look…I don't know if we have. I gave her some
advice that I'm heartily regretting now, because I think
she may be practising it—towards you.'

'Lydia, you struck terror into my heart when we first
met,' he said ominously, 'so—'

'I did not!'

'Yes, you did. You told me your sister was planning
to use me as a stud and that your father was liable to

come and harangue me, if nothing else. So what's in the wind now?'

Lydia sighed. 'I suggested, in the most general way, that perhaps she should play hard to get instead of being so…so generous towards the men she was sure she was in love with before she'd really had time to, well, know what it was.'

'So? That's good advice, I would have thought.'

She cast him a frustrated little glance. 'I think she's playing hard for *you* to get, Joe.'

He swore softly. 'Look, so long as you don't slap my face again, I admire your desire to save your sister from herself, if I may put it like that.' He stopped and their gazes caught and held.

Lydia bit her lip. 'I'm sorry for that, and it's not likely to happen again, but—'

'Yes,' he interrupted, 'there were other things said. But before we go into those, surely you must absolve me now from any of Daisy's—uh—problems?'

'I do,' she said, after a long pause. 'The one thing I can't get around is that she may be genuinely in love with you.'

'Oh, no,' he said grimly. 'No, Lydia. That's carrying your generosity towards your sister a bit too far. In fact it's more. It's cowardly, and I think you know why.'

'Here we go again,' she said, but with genuine distress in her voice as she put her mug down on the lawn and stood up. 'More insults, Joe? Well, I'm not going to listen to them. Goodnight.'

But as she went to walk away from him he was on his feet like a flash, then she heard his indrawn breath and saw his hands clench into fists before he deliberately relaxed and let them hang at his sides, and took a step backwards.

Surprise held her quite still, on two counts. The sheer intensity he'd conveyed before harnessing it, and the invisible cord of something flowing between them that refused to let her move away.

A cord that became a painfully searching moment as they stared into each other's eyes, and the power of knowing that he'd stopped himself from touching her against her will held her hostage, unable to move from the spot, she realised.

Then he said, barely audibly, 'Insulting is the last thing to describe my state of mind towards you. The fact that I seem to have two left feet is, in fact, an indication that I've been thrown off base from the moment I laid eyes on you and I don't seem to be handling it too well.'

'Oh, Joe.' She said it softly, on little more than a breath, and discovered she was moved by this admission, moved to a feeling of tenderness that made her reach out and put the tips of her fingers on the exact spot where she'd slapped him earlier.

He didn't stir for a long moment, but then he took her hand from his cheek and kissed the palm, and looked up into her eyes again. And she began to experience the unique sensation of drowning in that clever hazel gaze. Not only that, she thought with the edges of her mind, but drowning in a sudden surge of desire to be held and caressed and warmed by this surprising man who could also infuriate her like no other.

He did it slowly, as if testing her reaction bit by bit. He took the two steps that would bring them together but he was still only holding her hand. And the edges of her mind were slowly turning inwards, and everything else on it was dissolving into a feeling of helpless intimacy, a yearning to know again a man's hard strength against her, *this* man's. A yearning to be gathered close, and at the same time, a curiosity about how he would kiss her...

She should have known, she was to think later, that he would do it expertly and with finesse. She should have known that he would not rush but make sure she was following where he led with the lightest of touches that were at the same time devastatingly sensual. Even the way he slid her silver cardigan off and laid it over the chair involved the running of his fingers down her arms in a way that made her shiver with a kind of rapture.

Then he released her hair, and she shook her head so that it flew out in a cloud, then settled to its usual tousled unruly mane.

But there was no way she could have known the things he would say. No way of preparing herself to have her eyes, as he kissed her closed lids, her skin, as he laid his lips lightly on her slender neck, her hair, as he ran his hands through it luxuriously, or her body, as he ran his hands down it, described so richly and beautifully in his deep murmur.

Nor could she have predicted that beneath the weight of his words and his hands, she would feel like an exquisite creature instead of a rather gangly vet, with skin that felt like velvet and had the glow of crushed pearls, sapphire eyes, a graceful, slender figure that was beckoning him from behind a sheer veil of star-dusted georgette without the benefit of its satin lining.

'You kissed the Blarney Stone somewhere along the line, Joe,' she whispered once, in an effort to keep her feet on the ground—speaking metaphorically? she wondered at the same time.

'No, I'm kissing you, Lydia,' he murmured. 'Did you know your skin has a perfume all of its own? *Fragrance*

Lydia, I'll call it. And I love the fact that you're tall enough not to give me a crick in my neck when we do this...'

'This', when they'd stopped smiling, was to come together again, so she was deep within his embrace with her breasts crushed against him as they kissed once more, and the stirrings of desire were flowering within her as she slid her arms around his waist and moved against him.

What would have happened to them from there on she couldn't doubt, because amidst the embarrassment that ensued there was also the cruel little feeling of a cold, empty space within. But the fact of the matter was the homestead party chose that moment to return, and she and Joe Jordan were surprised, if not exactly *in flagrante delicto*, certainly in a telling embrace.

As a chorus of whistles erupted his arms hardened around her and he swore beneath his breath. Then he took one arm away, but kept her close, saluted the revellers leisurely and drew her around the corner of the house out of sight.

'How... ? Oh, no,' she said, distraught, with her hands to her hot cheeks. 'What will Sarah think?'

'She's probably cheering. Don't be upset. Let's look on the funny side—'

'You may be able to; I can't see a funny side,' she broke in, then, to her amazement, started to smile, and finally they were laughing together. But as they sobered he took her hand and said her name.

She swallowed and shook her head, as if to clear her mind, but voices and footsteps were approaching and her nerve failed her.

'Goodnight, Joe,' she murmured, and fled.

*   *   *

The next morning her cardigan was folded neatly on a chair outside her verandah door with a spray of wild flowers resting on it.

But Lydia had had a night to come to her senses. She picked up the flowers and rested their soft, dewy petals against her cheek for a moment, then sighed and went to confront Joe Jordan, as well as his sister.

It didn't prove as awkward as she'd feared—Joe was already out on the run and Sarah was in such a fluster about leaving Katerina that the surprising events of the previous night seemed to have escaped her mind.

Finally, when Rolf was starting to look impatient and Pete was making remarks about them missing their Darwin connection because whilst he *was* flying them there it was not in a Lear jet, Lydia said to Sarah, 'Just go, Mrs Simpson! I'll look after the house, I'll clear up the shed, and between us Joe and I can fill in for you and Rolf.' She put her hands on Sarah's shoulders and added softly, 'Good luck.'

But when she wandered down to the shed it was to discover that Katerina's neighbours, now heading home either by road or air, had been very neighbourly. It was all tidied up.

Lydia leant against a metal upright and marvelled at the transformation. In the harsh daylight, and stripped of its streamers, music and greenery, its colourful revellers and the rich aroma of food, it was an ordinary, not particularly attractive tin shed. Was there an analogy there for her own situation? she wondered.

Had she been transported to a rich, sensuous wonderland by a clever man who could not be unskilled at pleasing women? Had he made her feel like a silken creature from the pages of an exotic *Arabian Nights* kind of story, which, of course, bore little resemblance to her down-to-earth, practical self? Not even Brad...

She stopped on the thought and put her hand to her mouth with something like anguish piercing her heart. How could she compare them? How could a physical attraction take the place of that sense of belonging, that ease she and Brad had had? That feeling of knowing Brad through and through, whereas Joe Jordan was an enigma and sometimes a dangerous one.

To complicate matters, she mused, after staring into the distance rather blindly, she couldn't now blame him for assuming she was a willing participant in the sensual games they'd played last night—and she was stuck on her own with him for the next three weeks.

She moved at last and decided there was only one thing she could do at the moment, and that was to concentrate on earning her keep.

The gelding she usually rode was in the horse paddock, and as she whistled and produced the couple of sugar cubes she always put in her pocket it pricked its ears and trotted up obligingly. Stock horses were a breed in their own right in the outback, and although they'd suffered a decline in popularity when, for a variety of reasons, helicopter mustering had all but taken over, they were now coming back into their own, as were experienced ringers or coachers—quality riders skilled in handling mobs of cattle from horseback.

And Billy, her chestnut gelding, was a joy to ride. She could never compare herself in skill or quality to most of the ringers she'd seen on Katerina, but with Billy's help, his training and stamina, she'd managed not to disgrace herself. It had been Joe who'd picked Billy out for her and recommended her to put herself in his hands...

'He knows what he's doing,' he'd said, with a glimmer of a smile.

She'd later discovered that Joe himself had broken Billy in. One of the many surprising discoveries she'd made about the man she'd labelled as 'trendy' on first impressions, she reflected, as she put the heavy stock saddle on and tightened the girth, then crammed her felt hat on and swung herself up on to the horse. Another being the fact that he could ride like the wind with the best of them and was obviously respected, not only as an owner of Katerina but for his skills.

She guided Billy out of the paddock, opening and closing the gate without having to dismount, and set him at a canter towards the portable yards that they'd erected for the latest muster.

After a while she was able to drag her mind from Joe Jordan as her body rose and fell to the rhythm of the canter, the saddle creaked and a light breeze lifted Billy's mane. She gazed about as she rode and noticed that the countryside was drying out noticeably as winter slid towards the wet season. A swirl of dust on the horizon showed her that the delayed road train was crawling along a rocky track towards another swirl of dust— the temporary yards. She slowed Billy to a walk, not that keen to arrive, and not only because of Joe, but because of a sense of wonder at her environment.

Despite feeling like a dot in the vast sandy-pink landscape, she didn't feel intimidated. Which was a little strange, because she'd lived all her life in a city. Of course her father had taken both she and Daisy on pilgrimages to the bush, and perhaps his preoccupation with it had encouraged this attraction for her. But that still didn't explain the feeling she'd discovered since coming to Katerina of a better understanding of what life was about, although how or why she wasn't sure.

Did it mean she felt more at peace with herself because of these surroundings? Was it the challenge she enjoyed? It certainly wasn't always comfortable. Despite most modern amenities at the homestead there was still the heat, the dust, there were still the flies, the loneliness of the wet months when roads were impassable and the only way in and out was by air.

She shrugged and clicked her tongue and wondered, as Billy lengthened his stride, whether it was all much simpler. She was restless because of the lack of focus in her life...

As soon as she arrived at the yards, it was plain to see things weren't going well. The cattle truck, a monster with two double-decker trailers, had somehow managed to jackknife in its attempt to back up to the loading ramp and jam one of its couplings. Fortunately, it was a smallish muster, this one, and the drafting process had gone smoothly, so it was only the sale cattle still yarded. But the dust and the delay were making them restless, and, not long after she arrived, they broke through the fence.

She thought later that Billy had acted instinctively, and it had to have helped that she'd been the only one mounted whilst all the other men had been labouring over the truck. All the same it took her breath away when the horse took off at a gallop and began to round up the errant cattle.

She regained her breath and had the sense to simply sit tight for a while, but then she began to participate, to move with him, to rip her hat off and use it as well as the whistles and hand signals she'd learnt over the previous weeks—a whole language of hand signals that were vital when you were working as a team. And there were others on their horses now, helping as they attempted to calm and collect a mob of cows bent on stampeding to freedom.

When they were all back in the yard, and Lydia was breathing raggedly and feeling exhausted, it was one of the ringers who said to her, 'Well done, missus! We'd'a lost 'em without you.'

She patted Billy's steaming neck and slid off him. 'I think it was my horse, but thanks.'

Joe strode up to her as she hit the ground and found herself curiously unsteady on her legs. He put his hands around her waist, smiled into her eyes, and murmured, 'I could kiss you for that, Ms Kelso. I haven't been having the best of days, as you can see.' And he did.

Whereupon everyone cheered and someone called out, 'I'd ride her straight to the altar if I were you, Joe. Word's around you two got something going, and it's 'bout time you got hitched, anyway.'

'Steak, eggs, chips and a salad?'

'Why not?' Joe responded to her query re dinner. 'But only if you promise to sit down first and tell me what you're thinking.'

They hadn't come back together. Joe had insisted she hitch a ride on a vehicle bound for the tool shed not long after her daring feat of mustering, and had promised to lead Billy home himself. So she'd spent the rest of the day making sure the vet station was in good order, then she'd walked up to the homestead and, as she'd promised Sarah, tidied up there.

He had only just come in when she'd posed the question of dinner to him. So that while she was showered, changed and looking cool and clean in a pair of grey trousers and a warm blue long-sleeved shirt, he was the opposite. His khaki shirt was sweat-soaked and clinging to his back, the golden hairs on his arms were invisible beneath a layer of dust, and his hair, as he took his hat off, was plastered to his head.

'Nothing very much,' she responded casually, with a friendly smile. 'Well, I just thought I'd check your preferences for dinner so you can go and have a heavenly shower while I get started. I'm sure you're dying for a beer, but it will go down much better when you're cleaned up.'

He stood in the middle of the kitchen, staring at her narrowly. Then he said slowly, 'Is this what I think it is?'

She looked at him blankly.

'Get back into your box, Fido, in other words?'

'I don't know what you mean—' She broke off and closed her eyes briefly, because of course she knew exactly what he meant. She'd also underestimated her capacity to deal with him in what she'd hoped would be a friendly but firm manner.

'Lydia?'

She moved towards the stove, unable to think of a thing to say and unable to meet the challenge in his eyes.

'All right,' he drawled, 'but I not only need a shower, I need about an hour to make some calls and send some faxes. If you'd like to have dinner ready then, I'll join you.'

He strode out of the kitchen, leaving Lydia so angry she could only stare after him, speechless. What was going through her mind was quite articulate, however. How dared he treat her as if she were only the hired cook?

It was because she desperately needed something to

do that she did in fact cook dinner, although with an angry reluctance as she pondered his sheer high-handedness. It also occurred to her that she should have known he could assume this manner. She'd seen it with her own eyes today down at the muster yards, although she'd failed to take heed. But with Rolf gone, Joe had gone up a notch, in a manner of speaking.

His authority had always been there, she reflected, but in a low-key way so that his manager, who also happened to be his brother-in-law and a shareholder, was his equal. Now he deferred to no one, and if she hadn't been dazzled by him on another plane, as well as trying to sort out philosophical questions to do with her own life, she would have taken heed of his manner today down at the yards—very much the boss and respected for it.

But not by her, she thought, as she dished up dinner, set it out in the verandah room, called out that it was ready, and sat down to start without waiting for him.

He came within a few minutes, and, without consulting her, opened a bottle of wine and poured two glasses.

She stared at the glass he'd placed in front of her. 'Don't imagine this will soften me up, Joe.' And she raised deep blue hostile eyes to his.

He shrugged and sat down. 'All right. Let's have a good row, Lydia. If we're going to spend the next three weeks together, we might as well clear the air now.'

He'd changed into a green and white checked viyella shirt and fawn corduroy trousers. He looked aggressively clean and scrubbed and exuded the faint tang of soap. He also looked attractive in that lean-hipped, broad-shouldered way that was a trial to many woman, she had no doubt, and looked dangerous at the same time—as only he could.

'You can go first,' he added casually, and started to cut his steak.

'No, I've a better idea. Why don't you? I haven't got much to say—how *can* you?' she added, as if genuinely offended, with her gaze on the tomato sauce bottle he'd just upended over his chips.

'I may be a gourmet in some respects but that's how I like my chips, Lydia. With tomato sauce.' He put the bottle down with a small thump.

'My apologies,' she murmured dryly.

He looked at her sardonically.

'You may not realise this, Joe,' she said through her teeth, 'but I am not the hired household help. I'm doing this out of the goodness of my heart, so don't think you can order me around as to when I deliver meals because you might just find yourself getting your own!'

'And you may not realise *this*, Lydia, but when you kiss someone the way you did last night, it is then unacceptable to treat them as if it never happened, with a pat on the head and—'

'Joe, nevertheless,' she said with an effort, 'we need to put it into perspective. I'm just not prepared to carry on mindlessly. Nor do I appreciate the whole world linking me with you.'

He raised an eyebrow. 'A very small world. And have I asked you to carry on *mindlessly*?'

Lydia helped herself to some salad. 'Well, no...but you did kiss me without my permission in front of a lot of people today,' she finished, with more spirit.

There was so much irony in his hazel gaze when she looked across at him at last that she bit her lip and looked away immediately, knowing she was perceptibly flustered.

'Other than that, then, is there anything about me...'

he paused, then continued in a leisurely way which she found insulting '…that tells you I can't understand the dilemma you're facing?'

'What do you mean?'

He smiled without amusement. 'The dilemma of how to say goodbye to an old love and start a new one.'

Shock made Lydia stare at him with her lips parted.

'And is that because you've decided, for some reason, that I'm particularly insensitive?' He posed the question blandly.

She swallowed and could think of nothing to say.

'If it's not that,' he murmured, looking at her narrowly and with sheer arrogance, 'are you clinging to the Casanova view of me for a very good reason—you're afraid you'll go overboard otherwise?'

'If you don't stop making fun of me you're liable to find yourself not only without a cook but without a member of the mustering team,' she said sharply, and clashed her knife and fork together over her unfinished meal.

'Then let's talk, Lydia. What is the problem?'

'If you must know, you hit the nail on the head twice. I *was* thinking of Brad today, and I *don't* know whether you're a Casanova—but you seem to have got to thirty-two with no commitments, and you do some things most professionally, so—'

'Would you rather I was clumsy and mauled you?' he asked with dangerous irony.

Lydia chose to ignore this taunt as she looped her hair behind her ears. 'And you also told me you had no intention of marrying anyone at the moment, least of all my sister.'

'Well, why the hell can't we discuss these things?' he said grimly.

'Because what I felt for Brad was very special and very private.' She stopped abruptly.

'Go on.'

'And what I feel for you...' Her shoulders slumped. 'It doesn't seem to be the same kind of thing. I don't know you through and through; I don't even know if I can trust you.'

'If you're expecting me to leap on you and have my way with you without your permission, Lydia, it's a vain hope, my dear. I don't operate that way,' he drawled.

She tightened her lips, then managed to say smoothly, but with obvious scorn, 'That's the other thing. That kind of superficial cleverness doesn't appeal to me in the slightest. In fact you annoy me much more than you...than the other thing.'

'One wouldn't have thought so from your performance last night.'

Lydia pushed her chair back and stood up. 'Go to hell, Joe Jordan,' she whispered. 'And don't expect me to do the dishes!'

The next few days were spent in a sort of armed truce.

They had a bit of breather before the next muster but that didn't mean there was any idleness on Katerina Station. Running road repairs were made with the huge grader, fences and dams were checked—all sorts of maintenance work was carried out, and carried out quickly and competently for a boss who was, visibly, not in the best of moods.

Lydia took the time to devote herself to the horses, most of which were turned out for a few days' rest. She treated them for internal parasites, checked them for any sign of lameness, loose teeth, and operated on one to remove a malignant sun spot. She was also able to cure a case of colic, which could lead to a twisted bowel and be fatal for a horse.

She also got to know a bit more about the running of Katerina homestead as well as the station. Because the nearest shop was a day and half's drive away, it was critical to ensure not only foodstuffs but fuel and so on were kept up. This had been Sarah's responsibility, listing and ordering the supplies by the fortnightly truckload.

Of course they had their own meat—an unlimited supply, if you could stomach beef every day of the week—which was killed on the property, and there was a retired ringer who looked after the homestead garden and, according to the seasons, produced vegetables and had a flock of chickens he guarded with his life from snakes and dingoes. All the rest had to be brought in.

Although they didn't say much, she felt again the growing respect of the men she worked with, although there were occasions, when Joe was being extra terse, that she was on the receiving end of some odd little glances. No one on Katerina seemed to have any doubt as to what the cause of his unfriendly mood was.

She also exercised Sarah's two jumpers daily, and in any spare time she had looked after the homestead, probably giving it more attention than Sarah did. And she consulted with Sammy, the retired ringer, because she was a gardener at heart, and this little oasis in the middle of the bush fascinated her.

When they did meet on their own, she and Joe, which was only at meal times, and only rarely, because he left the house before sunrise and returned late so most of his meals were kept hot for him and he ate them in his study, she was as normal as she could be whilst uttering the least she could. Although polite, he in turn contrived to make her feel as if she didn't exist. Apart from one occasion…

One of the cattle dogs cornered a wild pig and got itself severely gored. Sammy came to get her, but when she arrived at the vet station Joe had made the decision that the kindest thing to do for the dog was to put it out of its misery.

'Oh, no you don't,' she said coolly. 'I can handle this.'

'Lydia—'

She straightened from her examination of the dog. 'Joe, you could help if you want to or you could go away, but don't tell me how to do my job!' She opened her own bag and took out a McGill tube with an inflatable cuff to insert into the dog's windpipe, a respirator bag, and prepared an anaesthetic. She scrubbed up, pulled on gloves and set out her pre-sterilised instruments.

Joe was still there.

'If you're going to stay, I'll tell you how to use the respirator bag if we need it. Please do exactly as I say.'

An hour later she'd repaired a tear to the animal's abdominal wall and trimmed and sutured a lung as well as stitching some superficial gashes. Joe had followed her directions while she'd been working on the lung to the letter.

'There.' She wiped her brow with her sleeve, stripped off her gloves and scrubbed her hands again. 'In a few days he should be as good as new.'

'I'll nurse him.' Sammy stepped forward. 'Just tell me what to do, but I got a good hand with crook animals.'

She told him, but promised to check him out herself

frequently. She then eyed Joe Jordan, who was watching her broodingly, and walked out.

She didn't see the way he noted how she looped her hair behind her ears, a trademark gesture she always made when under any kind of pressure, and had no way of knowing what was going through his mind.

Girl, woman, married *woman,* Joe found himself thinking. *Cool, dedicated vet, deadly with your tongue but sometimes, when you walk away from me with that boyish stride, so slim and serious, I don't know what the hell to make of you, Lydia Kelso. But if you still want war, if you still like to think you're in charge, so be it!*

And their polite but armed truce continued.

Despite the incongruity of it, and despite asking herself why she stayed on and telling herself it was for Sarah's sake, Lydia couldn't help wondering whether she was holding out for a moral victory of sorts. As in trying to make the point that he was being ridiculous?

But, being on the whole honest with herself, she was aware that she'd been the one to force this kind of impasse on them. She just hadn't expected him to take her at her word so literally, which was not a comforting thought to take to bed with her.

Four days after their initial fall-out, she had to admit that she, her nerves, or something, had been worn down, to the extent that she was possessed of the desire to scream at him that she was not a complete stranger who cooked his meals and looked after his animals.

Whether she would have done it she was never to know, because they bumped into each other that evening as she was on her way to bed and he was coming out of his study.

It was a particularly cold night and she had on warm

pyjamas under her violet velvet robe. She was also clutching a hot water bottle wrapped in a towel.

He said nothing after a searching glance up and down her, and stood aside for her to pass.

But it struck Lydia that he looked particularly grim, even slightly pale beneath the overhead light, and she didn't move. 'Is…is something wrong?' she asked tentatively.

Once again that hazel gaze dwelt on her. And it was so unreadable and his mouth so hard she tensed and wondered what kind of a put-down to expect.

What came was the last thing she expected. He said, 'I've just had a call from Sarah. She and Rolf are splitting up.'

CHAPTER FIVE

'BUT...but *why*? I thought—I thought they...' Lydia stopped helplessly.

'Thought they were the ideal couple?' he supplied.

She stared at him, with her mind reeling. Then she said, 'Would you like a cup of coffee?'

His leant his head back against the wall and she saw the lines scored beside his mouth. 'Thanks,' he said after a moment.

She made a pot of coffee and they sat in the kitchen, which was warmer than the rest of the house. She warmed her hands on her mug and shook her head dazedly. 'I suppose I didn't really stop to think about it. He's not that easy to know, Rolf, is he? He doesn't say much and I guess I thought if he wasn't overtly demonstrative it just wasn't his nature—did you expect this?' she asked directly, with a frown. 'I remember you saying something now—about Sarah thinking she had him housetrained—but...' She shrugged.

Joe sighed. 'I've been afraid for a while that it was in the wind.'

'Because of her inability to conceive?' Lydia said, and looked shocked. 'But that's why they went away—oh, the poor thing,' she whispered.

'No—well,' Joe amended, 'it may have been a factor, but for quite some time I've been aware of another worm of discontent niggling away at Rolf. He likes to be his own boss. He's not happy with a half-share in Katerina; he would like he and Sarah to have the lot. Unfortunately, we had differing opinions on a couple of critical issues, and Sarah voted with me.'

'Oh.' It was one little word she uttered but it conveyed a wealth of understanding.

'As you say,' he agreed.

'Why did she? I mean, were they such contentious issues and was Rolf...wrong? He seemed like the consummate cattleman, if you don't mind me saying so.'

Joe grimaced. 'It wasn't a question of being right or wrong about cattle *per se*. It was a question of expanding Katerina. It was a question of perhaps getting out of our depth financially. That's how I saw it, anyway, and so did Sarah, who can be quite shrewd at times.'

'So—but why did it all boil up like this?' Lydia asked.

'I don't know if he picked his timing deliberately; I don't think so. Perhaps the reality of the *in vitro* programme hit him all of a sudden. But anyway, the state of play is, either I buy their share, so they can get a place of their own, or we dissolve the partnership and he sells his share elsewhere and leaves Sarah.'

'But you were so good with him!'

He raised an eyebrow at her.

'I mean, I was only thinking the other day that you were a team, you and Rolf, whereas on your own you're a different matter.' She paused.

'As in how?' he asked.

'Very much the boss,' she said flatly, after a moment.

He smiled fleetingly. 'I take it you don't approve?'

She favoured him with a straight, give-nothing-away gaze, then shrugged as if it were neither here nor there. 'So, when Sarah married Rolf, did she—did either of you—have any inkling this was likely to happen?'

'Women in love, certainly in the first flush of love, are not renowned for their intuition. No,' he said, as

Lydia made an abrupt movement, 'let me finish. Sarah *was* madly in love with Rolf, and quite blind to the fact that she might not be able to handle him in this kind of situation. I know, because I tried to point it out to her.'

Lydia subsided, although reluctantly. Then she thought for a bit and said finally, 'Could—is there any way they could buy you out?'

'They'd have to borrow heavily. But that's assuming I want to be bought out.'

She glanced at him. 'I just thought—you do seem to be in two minds about whether you're a cartoonist or a grazier.'

'Perhaps,' he responded. 'And, sure, I've had the best of both worlds for quite a while now, but to a certain extent that was to accommodate Sarah and Rolf. I've never had any intention of giving up Katerina, however.' He got up and walked over to the stove to refill his cup from the gently bubbling percolator, then leant against the counter.

Lydia shivered involuntarily, because there was something quite implacable about Joe Jordan at that moment, although he'd spoken evenly and without emphasis. Not only implacable but tough, as he leant negligently against the counter with his legs crossed and his arms folded. She wondered if it might be his olive-green military-style ribbed pullover with elbow and shoulder patches and his khaki trousers that contributed to this impression, but immediately doubted it from the set of his jaw.

'What is going to happen, then?' she asked.

He shrugged. 'It's up to Sarah. She says she's told Rolf she can't agree to what he wants. I told her to think again. Men are... It *can* be hard to play second fiddle. And if Rolf is that kind of man, she won't be able to change him. That doesn't mean to say all the other things she loves about him, or did, count for nothing.'

'It's a choice between Katerina or Rolf for her, then,' Lydia said abstractedly. 'She does seem to love this place.'

'Yes,' he agreed, 'but whether it will be the same when she's on her own, without Rolf, is another matter. And Katerina, while I'm here, will always be here for her.'

'Could you buy them out?'

'With a bit of manoeuvring, yes.'

She blinked at him. 'Is cartooning that well paid?'

A spark of amusement lit his eyes, although he said gravely, 'It's very well paid, as it happens, when you make a name for yourself, but I—er—happen to have other resources.'

Curiosity made her say without thinking, 'Such as?'

This time he laughed softly. 'Are you compiling a dossier on me by any chance, Lydia? If so, one has to wonder why?'

She bit her lip. 'Sorry, that was—I was just curious, but that was unforgivably nosy.'

He eyed her, still looking amused. 'I've been lucky enough to make some profitable investments and read the stockmarket fairly accurately.'

'So did Brad—' She broke off, and then, perhaps because she'd been so curious, added, 'Due to which I've been left rather...well off.'

'I'm glad,' he said simply.

She moved restlessly. 'It wasn't much consolation.'

'No.'

'What do you think Sarah will do? You know, now I come to think of it, I did notice Rolf looking impatient with her a couple of times.'

'I don't know what she'll do,' he said sombrely. 'You can never know exactly what goes on between a man and a woman, even if she's your sister. We'll have to wait and see.'

'You could be more tied to the place than ever,' Lydia said slowly.

'Sometimes these things have their chronological place in life.'

She looked at him with sudden interest. 'Do you mean Balmain and that kind of trendy life was starting to pall?'

He ran a hand through his hair and stroked his jaw thoughtfully. 'Perhaps. On the other hand there may always be a "Balmain" side of me, as you put it.' A glint of something lit his eyes—irony? she wondered. Because she'd misread him initially?

'But when you find yourself stopping what you're doing,' he went on, 'and missing your dog madly, when you find yourself picturing a sea of grass waving in the breeze and brolgas dancing beside a creek—a creek you've caught a barramundi in—and you can smell and taste and feel the bush as if it's singing to your soul—when that starts to happen fairly regularly it could be a message.'

'That's lovely.'

He smiled wryly at her. 'You may be more of a bushie at heart than you realise, Ms Kelso. You've certainly taken to it like a duck to water.'

'I know. I was asking myself only the other day what it was about, well, this life, I guess, that's so appealing.'

'Did you come to any conclusion?'

She was silent for a long moment. 'Not really, other than lacking a focus in my life.'

'Why don't you make me a focus?'

There was an even longer silence, during which the

only sound was Meg, changing her position in her basket.

'We've just been through the kind of domestic war for the last four days, Joe, that would make life hell for us, don't you think?'

He studied her comprehensively. From the fall of her hair, the lines of her face, that delicate yet stern mouth, down her velvet robe to her hands lying on the table. Upon one of which she always wore a man's signet ring. Brad's? he wondered.

He said, 'I don't know about you but that's because I'm as *frustrated* as hell.'

'And you don't think that could happen every time you don't get your own way?' she asked very quietly.

'There's only ever going to be one way to find out if we're soulmates, Lydia, and that's to get a bit closer,' he answered obliquely, but, of course, it was a telling comment.

She went to stand up, but stilled as he spoke again.

'If I've been difficult, you've been deliberately obstructive. You opened your heart just a little to let me kiss you, because you couldn't help it, then you closed all channels of communication like a clam. You even—' he smiled briefly '—decided to take issue with how I like my chips, as if I were untutored, uncultured and about ten years old. You know, there are times when you look about sixteen and times when you *do* act sixtyish.'

She licked her lips. 'Perhaps it's the only way I feel I can handle you, Joe.'

She saw his gaze narrow, then he pushed himself away from the counter almost carefully.

She didn't move as he came round the table slowly because she couldn't. It ran through her mind that the admission she'd made might not have been wise, and she might regret it, but at least it had been honest, and she couldn't help but feel she owed Joe Jordan that at least. If she'd hoped they could talk about it first—not that any of this had occurred to her as she'd spoken— she knew, as her heart started to thud irregularly, that it had been a faint hope at best, for them both...

Because something more powerful than talk was gathering them in faster than she could even think straight. His gaze had never left her face as he moved around the table, so it was with a slightly unsteady movement that he pulled out the chair beside her and sat down next to her, but facing her. All the same, he did talk.

'Don't look so wary,' he murmured. 'I'm neither the dentist nor a big bad wolf.'

She breathed unevenly, then had to smile. 'That makes me feel quite—silly.'

'Not at all. Wise girls take precautions. Don't give too much away; you never know what it can do to callow, impressionable people of the male sex,' he said gravely, but reached out and covered her hand with his.

'Joe, you're having me on!' But she was laughing a little now.

'Would I kid you?'

'Oh, yes,' she answered, 'but that's because you're rather—sweet.'

He looked instantly injured. 'I'm not that callow and impressionable!'

'Don't I know it.' Her eyes were dark blue and very bright.

'Then may I take another approach?' he said consideringly. 'Having once kissed you without your permission—'

'Twice.'

He shrugged. 'OK, twice, but anyway, may I have your permission now?'

'I guess I did ask for this,' she murmured, and leant forward to finger the lapel of his shirt.

'I wouldn't put it quite like that, but...' He released her hand and drew his fingers down her cheek. 'You did say something that made me a little mad with—hope? However, if you—'

'Joe Jordan, kiss me before I change my mind,' she advised, still laughing at him.

He did.

'That may have been a record,' he said solemnly, quite some time later.

Lydia brushed her hair with her fingers and tried to control her breathing. She was still standing within the circle of his arms, they were still in the kitchen, and although there was no enchanted garden around them, no star-spangled silk georgette dress between them, if Meg hadn't made a belated although timely intervention by getting out of her basket and coming over to investigate what they were doing, she would have been lost, she knew.

As it was, although they hadn't made the ultimate union, they'd come dangerously close. They'd imprinted the feel of their bodies on one another, he'd explored secret, sensitive sites and she'd melted beneath his lightest touch to a quivering rapture that she could no more disguise than fly to the moon. Because even beneath her pyjamas and robe he'd contrived to celebrate the slim, smooth planes and curves of her body in a way that made her feel unique.

She remembered saying once, 'If this is what you can

do in the middle of a kitchen, the mind boggles at the thought of a bed.'

To which he'd responded gravely, but with a sheerly wicked little glint in his eyes, 'I was also thinking how well we do this on our feet.'

'I...yes, that was quite something,' she murmured disjointedly, coming back to the present—and the realisation of how little control she had of herself in his arms.

He smiled fleetingly and touched a finger to her lips. 'Come.'

'Joe,' she whispered, and stopped.

He looked into her eyes, then took his arms away and tidied the top of her pyjama jacket, redid the sash of her robe around her waist, causing her to tremble because, with her tacit permission, his hands had found their way beneath both her robe and pyjamas and had wrought the most devastating delight on her bare breasts.

'I was only going to suggest we find somewhere more comfortable than the kitchen to sit down, and I was going to recommend a brandy to restore us to normality,' he said very quietly. 'That's all.'

She swallowed, then breathed more easily. 'That's...that would be nice.'

'So you see, Lydia,' he continued seriously although with a smile lurking in his eyes, 'I'm actually easier to handle in these circumstances than others.'

They went into the lounge and she sank into a comfortable armchair while he poured two balloon glasses of liqueur brandy. He also switched on a heater and brought it closer.

'Know what I think?' he said, after handing her a glass and sitting down on a footstool in front of her.

Lydia studied him, the slight hint of freckles, the way

his brown hair fell and the loose, twisted grace of his body hunched on the stool. 'No. What do you think, Joe?'

She was lying back in the chair with her head pillowed against the headrest and her glass cupped in her hands at the level of her slender waist. There were very faint blue shadows beneath her eyes, and still a slightly dazed air about her that caused him to grimace inwardly and wonder whether she was comparing him to her beloved Brad...

'I think we should go about this very carefully,' he said, studying his glass now, with his head bent, then lifting his hazel gaze to hers suddenly. 'I think there's only one criterion we should apply—that it exists in its own right, what we feel for and do to each other.'

'Yes,' she said after a long pause.

'I'm glad you agree.'

She sipped some brandy.

'All the same, I sense you have reservations,' he murmured.

She smiled briefly. 'I must be very transparent.'

'Tell me.'

'Joe...' She hesitated. 'How would you react if I told you it would be very easy to make you the focus of my life, especially in this setting?' She glanced around. 'But I can't help wondering how much the magic of the bush and Katerina is contributing to things.'

'You don't think that down in Balmain we would achieve record-breaking kisses?' he asked wryly.

She closed her eyes. 'Possibly.'

'So?'

'I can't think straight.' She moved her head restlessly against the back of the chair.

'Well, that's why I suggested we take things one at a

time. And my next suggestion is that you drink up and go to bed. You look exhausted.'

Lydia was silent for quite a while, then she said with a little glint of mischief dancing in her eyes, 'Is this Plan C, by any chance?'

He said gravely. 'Yes and no. It's certainly a device not to rush you or crowd you, as well as a way to get me to my own bed before I become—hard to handle. I guess Plan C is as good a name as any for it.' He shrugged.

She drained her glass and handed it to him. 'Then let us abide by your good intentions, Joe. Goodnight.' She stood up, but he remained still, although he watched her every move.

She hesitated, then kissed her fingers and touched them lightly to his brow, and went to bed.

Sleep didn't come easily, however. Memories of being in his arms, of responding to his touch, made her twist and turn restlessly. Memories of the extreme passion that had gripped them to the exclusion of all else—a man and a woman set alight by each other—but also memories of his forbearance and humour were on her mind. Such a change from the polite but cold stranger of the past four days, she thought.

At one point it was even hard not to admit that her lonely bed was lonelier and colder than she would have thought possible—lonelier and colder without a man who was not Brad.

Nor was she to know it was curiously prophetic that she should finally fall asleep with something her sister Daisy had said about Joe Jordan on her mind— *He's something else.*

Because, the next morning, who should fly into Katerina in a chartered light plane but Daisy herself?

* * *

Lydia was working in the garden when the plane buzzed over the homestead. She hadn't seen Joe that morning; he'd left before the crack of dawn. She got up off her knees and frowned, because it wasn't the station plane, she could tell by the markings, and it occurred to her that it might be Sarah. Because all the men were working on a new dam, she drove the utility down to the airstrip to pick up whoever it was, not for one moment expecting Daisy.

But Daisy it was, in jeans and a white silk blouse with elegant high-heeled boots, her dark hair loose and glorious and her violet eyes alight with love and laughter.

'Daisy!'

'I just couldn't resist surprising the life out of you, Lyd!' her sister responded joyfully, and flung her arms around her.

'You've certainly done that!' Lydia hugged her back. 'But—how come?'

'The Musica Viva tour! We've come to Darwin. I was so mixed up before you left, I hadn't even checked the itinerary properly. Then, when I got up here and discovered we had a couple of free days, I rang Chattie and got the details from her, and I chartered this little plane.'

She waved a hand towards the two-seater she'd climbed out of and explained she'd arranged with the pilot to fly her back to Darwin if there was any problem with her staying, otherwise he'd come back tomorrow to pick her up. 'Do you think they'll mind me staying a night, Lyd? I am your sister,' she finished anxiously.

'No. No! But...but there is one thing, Daisy.' Lydia stopped as the enormity of explaining hit her.

Daisy linked her arm through Lydia's as they walked towards the utility. 'Don't tell me I have to sleep rough; the house looked huge.'

'No. No, you won't. Daisy—Joe Jordan's here.'

Daisy stopped as if she'd been shot. Then she said breathlessly, 'How? Why? Does he have anyone with him? Lydia, I can't believe this!' And she was absolutely radiant.

'It turns out that he owns the place. Daisy, I have to confess something. I went to see him before I left, to make sure he wasn't playing fast and loose with you.'

Daisy blinked, then broke into spontaneous laughter. 'Darling, if you had any idea what lengths I went to—unsuccessfully—to get him to, well, take me seriously—' She broke off and shook her head. 'I can't believe you did that for me, but thanks. And I took your advice. I decided to play hard to get with him. Now I'll be able to tell whether it's worked. This is—amazing! I've got the feeling it must have been meant. The thing is, I can't stop thinking about him,' she added simply.

Neither can I... Lydia didn't say it, but the words seemed to burn themselves into her brain as she started the utility and prepared to drive her sister up to the homestead.

But she had to say something, and she had to say it soon. So her mind was working furiously while Daisy was obviously unaware of her preoccupation as she chattered about their father and Chattie and all the news from home.

Nor had any simple way of telling her sister the truth presented itself to Lydia when she drew up outside the garden fence and, to her horror, saw that the bull buggy was parked there, just arrived from the opposite direction, with Joe climbing out and Meg jumping off the back.

'Daisy,' she swallowed, 'Daisy—'

But Daisy forestalled her with a sigh of sheer wonder

as she said, 'He *is* quite something, isn't he?' and opened her door to get out.

'*Daisy,*' Lydia said desperately.

But Daisy said over her shoulder, 'Don't worry, darling! I'm still playing hard to get. Just watch me.'

So Lydia watched helplessly as her sister put on a bravura performance.

She advanced on Joe Jordan, who had stopped dead in his tracks, and put out her hand. 'Joe, I had no idea,' she said with obvious sincerity. 'I came to surprise Lydia because I'm in Darwin doing some concerts—you were the *last* person I expected to find here!'

Joe took her hand, although his gaze flicked briefly to Lydia, standing behind Daisy. All Lydia could do was shrug helplessly and make a negative gesture with her hands.

'I guess I could say the same,' Joe replied, shaking Daisy's hand. 'I thought it might be my sister Sarah flying in, that's why I came back, but—welcome to Katerina, Daisy. I'm sure Lydia is thrilled to see you.'

'Yes,' Lydia said, a touch belatedly although Daisy seemed not to notice.

'I'm only staying the night, if that's OK with you,' Daisy said charmingly to Joe. 'Truth to tell, a bit of a break from music is just what I need. We can...' She paused and looked at him seriously. 'We can still be friends, can't we?'

'Of course,' Joe Jordan murmured.

'Oh, good!'

It wasn't until Daisy had gone to bed that night that Lydia and Joe got the opportunity to talk in private.

They'd given Daisy a royal tour of the property. A flight over the next paddock to be mustered, a drive out

to the waterfall and pools for a swim, then a barbecue
under the stars with the mustering team. During it all
Daisy had been her own delightful self: bubbly, interested in all she saw, charming everyone she came in
contact with but showing not the slightest sign of any
personal interest in Joe.

Lydia had taken her a hot water bottle and stayed to
chat as Daisy got into bed, but it had not been for long
as her sister had yawned prodigiously several times and
laughingly admitted to being exhausted.

Joe was waiting for her in the kitchen when she went
back to it.

She pulled out a chair and sank down exhaustedly
herself.

'Here.'

'Thanks,' she murmured as he put a cup of tea in front
of her. 'Do I need this! What is it about tea in a crisis?'

He smiled faintly and sat down opposite with his own
cup. 'Is it such a crisis?'

'Yes,' she said baldly. 'I just couldn't find any way
to tell her.'

'But she genuinely had no idea she would find me
here?'

'None at all. I hadn't spoken to her, and I didn't mention it in my letters or when I rang Chattie.'

'Well, what is the crisis, then?' He watched her narrowly. 'She would appear to have given up on me.'

Lydia raised her dark blue gaze to his. 'It's as I feared.
She's playing hard to get. She can't stop thinking about
you.'

'Lydia—she *told* you this?'

Lydia nodded and sipped her tea.

'Then we'll just have to be honest.'

Lydia blinked a couple of times. 'That's easy to say, Joe, but—'

'No.' He slid his hand across the table and covered hers. 'This has gone on long enough. There is only one problem: that she's your sister. Believe me, Lydia, for all my sins, apart from wining and dining and escorting Daisy around a bit, I did not give her any reason to believe that there was more between us than friendship. I never laid so much as a finger on her intimately.'

'Joe—' Lydia held his gaze steadily '—don't you realise that wining, dining and escorting women around, even just a bit, leads to—expectations?'

'Of course.' He looked suddenly grim. 'But—and I've never told you this, because I know how defensive you are of Daisy—she was the one who did all the inviting. She was the one who rang me each and every time and suggested we do this, that or the other.' He gestured impatiently.

'You could have refused. Don't tell me you don't *know* the effect you have on women.'

'Yourself included?'

It wasn't the response she'd expected, and although she could tell that she'd angered him with what had been, perhaps, an unfair question, she felt her hackles rising all the same at the sheer arrogance of his expression as he sat opposite her, his hazel eyes supremely mocking and his mouth hard.

She pushed her cup away decisively and stood up. 'I'm not going to argue with you, Joe. Nor am I going to fall out with my own sister over a man I'm not even sure I like. Goodnight.'

'Before you go, Lydia, liking and loving are two different things. And there are some things I do to you that you actually appear to adore.'

'I'd hate to think how unchivalrous you could be if you really set your mind to it. I'm only surprised you haven't put it into a cartoon,' she said bitterly.

'Unchivalrous?' He raised an eyebrow at her. 'I was merely being honest. Think of it this way, though. Was it lonesome in your single bed last night? It sure as hell was in mine, and really,' he continued, softly but lethally, 'all the rest is insignificant, were *you* to be honest, Lydia.'

She walked out, but not before he'd seen the rise of rich colour in her cheeks.

She took a tea tray in to Daisy the next morning.

Her sister stretched luxuriously and propped herself up on the pillows. 'I slept like a log! Must be the country air. Thanks, you're a sweetie, but, hey!' She sat up and regarded Lydia with a frown. 'You don't look too bright—as if you didn't sleep a wink.'

'I did, but not many,' Lydia confessed, and sat on the twin bed as she poured the tea. 'There's something I have to tell you, Daisy, but first of all could you tell me this? Did Joe ever give you *any* hope that, well, something might come of your friendship, something more?'

Daisy blinked dazedly. 'You're not still worried about him playing fast and loose with me, Lyd? I—'

'Daisy, please, just tell me.'

Daisy pulled up the strap of her exquisite pearl silk nightdress, shrugged and gave the matter some thought. 'No,' she said finally. 'I mean I kept thinking he wouldn't want to go out with me if he didn't—well, you know, but...' She sighed suddenly. 'I was always the one who asked, and he was always the one who managed to turn it into a crowd.'

'So,' Lydia said slowly, 'when you thought to yourself

that this guy was something else and perhaps you should hang on to him, not just use him to father a child for you, he had never even—for example—kissed you?'

Daisy eyed her sister ruefully. 'No. I know what you're going to say. Am I mad or what? But the thing is—'

'I wasn't going to say that at all, because you see...' Lydia looked at her sister steadily, although she also swallowed a little painfully. 'He has kissed me.'

Daisy nearly dropped her cup.

And Lydia, with complete honesty, told her exactly what had happened between herself and Joe Jordan.

'Why didn't you tell me this yesterday?' Daisy whispered. 'I would have flown right back to Darwin there and then.'

Lydia rubbed her face wearily. 'I couldn't find the words. I'm so sorry—'

'No.' Daisy cast aside the bedclothes and came to sit on the twin bed beside her. 'I'm not blaming you for...anything, but I...even if I hadn't flown away I wouldn't have raved on about him. I...can't think straight,' she said.

'He's had that effect on me too,' Lydia commented with some cynicism as she recalled saying those exact words just two nights ago.

'So we've both fallen for the same man. No, no,' Daisy immediately corrected herself, 'there's no question of me *really* having fallen for him. It was just a bit of a pipe-dream—yes, that's all it was,' she assured Lydia.

Lydia put her arms around her. 'Is that why you couldn't stop thinking about him?' she asked gently.

'I will. I definitely will now,' Daisy promised. 'Look, you know me. I fall in and out of love at the drop of a hat. But you're different, and if you're finally getting over Brad and falling in love again then I'm the last person, the *very* last person, not to be happy for you! How can I make you believe it?' she asked with supreme anxiety.

Lydia hugged her again, and was silent for a time, hoping desperately that if nothing else the scales might have fallen from Daisy's eyes in regard to Joe. Then she said carefully, 'The thing is, he might not be the right man for either of us.'

'What do you mean?'

'I—' Lydia broke off, then started again. 'I don't know if it isn't just a physical attraction. There are times when I find him impossible. It's so different from how it was with Brad. We fight a lot.' She flinched inwardly, because it sounded awfully immature if nothing else.

Daisy said quietly, 'If a man wants to fight you and still make love to you, it's because there are obstacles he can't seem to overcome. And I would say Joe hasn't had a lot of opposition put in his way.' She grimaced. 'You have, sitting next to you, a perfect example. Would one of the obstacles you've been throwing up have been me, Lyd?'

'Of course. I've felt incredibly guilty. I tried, I really tried not to have anything to do with him, but—'

'Then things will be different from now on without that to worry about.'

'Is—the oboe player on the Musica Viva tour?' Lydia asked tentatively.

Daisy turned and smiled at her. 'No. But he sends me flowers every time we open in a new town. Now that I've Joe out of my system, who knows? I know!' She brightened. 'I shall tell Joe Jordan about him.'

'Daisy—'

But Daisy suddenly cast a wise little glance at her younger sister. 'No, I won't, but listen, kid.' They both smiled at the term Daisy had used over the years, then sobered. 'I need you to make me a promise. Don't hide behind me any longer. Whatever reservations you have about him, make sure they're genuine. Because I've retired completely from the lists—I was never in them in the first place, other than in my imagination.'

'But—'

'Lydia,' Daisy said, 'if you value me at all as a sister, if you understand that there are times when I'm rash because I can't seem to help myself but I'm *not* a complete fool who can't admit I do some crazy things, will you promise to banish all thoughts of me in the context of Joe Jordan?'

Lydia sniffed and blinked. 'I do value you as a sister. That's how I got myself into this in the first place,' she said huskily.

'So you promise?'

'OK. I promise.'

'Good. Because I'll tell you something else. I can't think why it didn't occur to me at the time—well, yes, I can—but I think he's just what you need...'

Daisy flew off after lunch.

Joe had come back from the dam to have lunch with them and no one would have guessed at all the dramatic strands threaded between them. Not that there had been anyone else to share their light-hearted lunch. Nor had Lydia any inkling that in the short time Joe and Daisy had been left alone, while she'd been dishing up the apple pie she'd made in the kitchen and whipping some cream, Daisy would turn the tables on her.

In fact, Joe was called away to a burst pipe they were

trying to connect from a bore to the dam as the plane
was taking off, so she went back to the homestead alone
and spent an uncomfortable afternoon wondering just
how she was going to handle Joe Jordan, and be handled
by him, in light of their 'words' of the previous evening.

Because, although she'd promised not to hide behind
her sister any longer, she was not about to drop her other
reservations about him. And while in her heart she could
no longer hide behind Daisy, she wasn't at all sure that
Joe deserved to know it.

She cooked roast beef and made a large pot of pumpkin soup. But it was quite dark and later than normal
before she heard the bull buggy pull up, and then she
nearly didn't recognise Joe when he loomed up on to the
verandah because he was coated in a mixture of dried
mud and grease.

'What…?' she began, but couldn't go on because he
looked so funny, and she started to laugh.

'You may well laugh, Ms Kelso,' he remarked bitterly, 'but if you'd spent the entire afternoon crawling
around a burst pipe and a faulty bore engine that re-
peatedly spouted when it wasn't supposed to and failed
to operate when it should have, you might be more sympathetic!'

'I'm entirely sympathetic, Joe. Entirely,' she protested. 'Just one thing, though. How are you going to
get clean without reducing the bathroom to a sea of mud
and grease?'

He threw his hat on to a chair and put his hands on
his hips. 'I have no intention of doing that to a bathroom.
What do you think I am?'

'I won't answer that.' She grinned. 'So?'

'For my sins—all sorts of sins I've never committed,
by the way—I shall have to use the tank shower. Which,

you may or may not know, is cold. Freezing, to be more accurate. Would you mind, if it wouldn't be too much trouble, getting me a towel and a piece of soap?' He removed his hands from his hips and started to unbutton his shirt.

'On the double, sir!' Lydia responded smartly, and disappeared inside.

When she returned he'd dispensed with his shirt and the overhead verandah light was mellow on the clean skin beneath it, on the smooth flow of muscles across his shoulders and the sprinkling of golden hairs on his chest that turned darker and became thicker towards his waist.

He stopped with his fingers on the waistband of his trousers, she stopped on the doorstep almost as if she'd been shot and for about half a minute, they made a frozen little tableau with their gazes clashing—once she'd been able to tear hers from the sleek, beautiful proportions of his body.

Then Lydia came to life and advanced towards him. 'Soap, a towel—two towels actually—and—this.'

The last thing she handed him was an open bottle of beer. Their fingers brushed as he took it and she took her hand away rather quickly. 'Just thought it might help,' she murmured, 'while you're out there in the dark, showering under the tank stand.' She stopped speaking, because it sounded more like babbling than coherent speech to her, and she retreated to the doorstep.

Joe studied the beer bottle, then raised it to his mouth and took several long swallows. He shuddered as it went down, then looked across at her. 'You were right. You never know, I might even be able to sing during this bracing experience.' He turned away, vaulted off the verandah and disappeared into the darkness.

Lydia stood where she was for a moment longer experiencing several reactions. Relief that the ice had been broken was one, but the comfort that brought to her was tempered somewhat because she'd been reduced to feeling like a starstruck girl on a very physical level.

Then she heard him—singing in a deep baritone that carried clearly as the sound of water rushing could also be heard. Although—and she guessed this was as he came into contact with the tank water—the baritone rose to a distinct yodelling falsetto for a moment, before continuing rather breathlessly.

She laid her cheek on the doorjamb and laughed until tears sprang to her eyes. Then she went away to co-ordinate dinner.

CHAPTER SIX

IT WAS an almost frighteningly alive Joe Jordan who sat down to dinner presently.

If she'd been struck by him on the verandah without his shirt, she was doubly struck, she thought ruefully, by the impact of his clean, vigorous masculinity as he sat opposite her in the verandah room. He'd put on a grey tracksuit, his hair gleamed smooth and neat, and just below the surface lay all the power of a strong man in his prime plus that sheer sex appeal.

Was he altogether aware of it? she wondered. What was it precisely—and how many times had she asked herself that? A tall, supple body, to be sure, but there had to be more. A vitality about him and his sense of humour. The undoubted and, much as she hated to admit it, clever arrogance he could exhibit at the same time as you sensed that the single-minded attentions of Joe Jordan could be the pathway to a certain kind of heaven—as she not only sensed but now knew to be true.

She dished up the pumpkin soup as all this passed through her mind and passed him the croutons.

'I'm starving,' he announced. 'And if that's roast beef, my dear Lydia—' he gestured towards the sideboard and a covered dish set on a heating pad '—you have won my heart.'

Lydia sat down and picked up her soup spoon. 'You seem to be in a very good mood, Joe,' she murmured, then winced to think she could have made any reference to their dispute of the previous evening. 'For a man who's been battling wayward bores and pumps.'

He glinted her an enigmatic little look that told her all the same that he'd noticed her movement of regret. 'As a matter of fact I'm a man in a unique position.'

'Oh?'

'Yep.' He continued to drink his soup.

'So you're not going to tell me,' she said.

He looked up, and this time his glance was entirely readable; it was about as wicked as she'd ever seen. 'You may not approve,' he warned.

She pushed her plate away and asked ominously, 'Have you been having bets with yourself again?'

'No, ma'am! I learnt that lesson the hard way.'

Lydia plucked her napkin from her lap and dropped it on to the tablecloth from a height. 'Joe, that is not true!'

He looked surprised. 'I can assure you it is—'

'You know very well what I mean—you were the one who—stopped.' She stopped herself, appalled at the admission she'd made, then tossed her head as if to stand by what she'd said.

Something—could it have been oddly tender?—lit his hazel eyes for a moment before he said, 'Meg was the one to take any credit the night before last.'

'A lot of men would have pressed on.'

'They may not have heard about Plan C.'

A smile trembled on her lips. 'You're impossibly…nice sometimes, Joe.'

'Well—' he shrugged '—that's a relief. I thought you were going to say something else. Impossibly sweet.'

She laughed openly, then said curiously, 'So what was it if not a bet?'

He finished his soup and stood up. 'Would you like me to carve?'

'Please,' she murmured, and gathered the soup plates.

He lifted the lid on the roast, inhaled luxuriously and passed the carving knife over the steel a couple of times before he said, 'I'm in the unique position of having been warned by each of the Kelso sisters to be on my best behaviour towards the other sister.' He cut the beef expertly and placed a faintly pink slice, a perfect example of rare roast beef, on a plate.

'I…you…Daisy *told* you!'

'Daisy warned me that if I hurt you I would have her to contend with,' he corrected. 'By the way, I admire your courage in coming clean with her. I know I recommended it, but I never for one minute thought it would be easy, although there was never any question of you stealing me from her.'

Lydia swallowed several times, then accepted a plate from him and took the lid off the vegetables. 'What exactly did she say?' she asked in a strangled sort of way.

He sat down again with his own plate and helped himself to gravy. Then he looked at her completely soberly. 'She didn't tell me anything I didn't know, except, perhaps, to underline what a perfect couple you and Brad Kelso had been. And how difficult it was for you to forget him.'

'Oh.'

'She also gave me a few words of wisdom to do with myself.' He raised his eyebrows.

'Such as?'

'"Don't imagine you're the best thing since sliced bread, Joe Jordan."'

Lydia gasped. 'Daisy said that to you?'

'Uh-huh.' He cut some beef into a triangle and studied it before putting it into his mouth.

Lydia stared at him dazedly. 'Was she joking, was she angry, or what?'

He finished his mouthful then reached for a glass of water. 'It would appear she's suffered a complete reversal of feeling for me. No—' he grinned fleetingly at Lydia's expression '—she was very honest. She said she'd been a fool and she'd caused unnecessary complications between you and I but it was all over for her. All the same—' he gestured '—that's when she mentioned the sliced bread bit.'

'What did you say to her?' Lydia asked, with a mixture of dread and fascination.

He looked over her head, as if trying to recall his exact words. 'I said it had been an honour to know her because in her own way she was unique, and if I hadn't known her, I wouldn't have known you. I think Daisy and I understand each other now.'

'Oh.'

'That's the third time you've said that, Lydia.' He looked at her wryly.

She shook her head. 'I feel as if I'm lost at sea without a chart.'

'So do I.'

Lydia blinked at him.

'The thing is…' He paused and looked at her reflectively. 'If you really want to dedicate your life to the memory of Brad, I wouldn't be so crass as to take issue with that.'

Lydia licked her lips. 'Was that something else Daisy indicated?'

'No. In all conscience, though, I felt I had to say it.'

'Thank you,' Lydia whispered, then cleared her throat

to go on normally. 'The thing is, I don't know. Yes, I do,' she contradicted herself immediately. 'Although there'll always be a corner of my heart for him, I've made no pact to dedicate my life to a memory.'

'Is that,' he said slowly, 'a go-ahead, Lydia?'

She tried to compose her thoughts. 'It's an admission,' she said at last, 'that you intrigue me, annoy me, set me alight—but more than that? I can't say at this stage.'

He grinned ruefully. 'Very succinct,' he commented. 'It just about sums up how I feel about you, too.'

Lydia suffered the sensation of having the wind rather taken out of her sails, and gritted her teeth on a tart retort. He'd be quite entitled to point out that what was sauce for the goose was sauce for the gander, and being Joe Jordan no doubt would, should she give him the opportunity.

'You were going to say?' he asked innocently, right on cue.

'Nothing. Except this is one of the moments when you're annoying me, but I'll leave you to work out why. Have you heard anything from Sarah?'

He registered the deliberate change of subject with the flicker of a smile but said soberly, 'No. I'm going to try to get hold of her tonight. I really thought she was Daisy, if you know what I mean, and I didn't know whether to be happy or sad for her.'

'Joe, I don't want to add to your problems, but I took six weeks' leave from my job in Sydney and there's only a few weeks left now. Not that I've been much help over the past few days, but—'

'Not your fault,' he broke in. 'And we've only got a few more paddocks to muster. With some help from above we may get it done in a fortnight.'

'I noticed the other day how the country was drying out,' she said.

'By the time the monsoon starts in November or December we're generally desperate for rain,' he commented. 'That's how it goes in this part of the world, a feast or a famine. Talking of which, did I see a lemon meringue in the kitchen?'

'I'll get it.'

But he wandered through to the kitchen himself as she was serving up two portions of the lemon meringue instead of bringing it out to the table. And he put his hands on her waist from behind.

She stilled, then put the cake slice down and turned to face him. 'What?' she breathed.

'Don't you know?' He raised a hand and trailed his fingers down the side of her neck.

She shivered, but not because she was cold. She had on her warm blue long-sleeved shirt, with jeans. 'Yes, I know,' she said barely audibly. 'And I have been lonesome the last two nights.'

'But it's a big step?' he suggested.

She swallowed, and nodded.

He touched his lips to her forehead, then said into her hair, 'It is for me too.'

Surprise held her rigid for a moment, then she put her hands on his upper arms and he looked down into her eyes.

'You can't mean that, Joe?'

'Why not?' he murmured. 'I feel like a rookie upstart with you sometimes, Lydia.' His hands were on her waist again. 'A playboy, a rather shallow sex object, slickly clever, definitely lightweight in the commitment department having reached the grand old age of thirty-two—'

'I didn't put it all quite like that.'

'You gave me to understand it, however.' He shrugged and stroked her hair, confusing her all the more. 'Then there was the way you amazed me when you got up here. You showed an awful lot of courage for a city girl, you are obviously a very professional vet and I know enough about vets to know you need an awful lot of brains to get into it in the first place. Whereas all I demonstrated was that I could be a very volatile artist of sorts. So, yes, that added to my feeling of inferiority.'

Lydia could only stare at him with her lips parted.

He smiled slightly and traced the outline of her mouth with his forefinger. 'But most of all,' he said very quietly, 'and this is why it would be a big step for me, Lydia, you've known—perfection. I never have. Not the kind that's locked me to a lover both mentally and physically.' He paused. 'Even in the relationships I've had, I was always—it was as if I was standing on the outside, waiting for it to happen.'

She blinked dazedly.

'Which has left me wondering,' he went on, 'whether the lack is something within me.'

'So you don't think you've ever been in love?' she asked huskily.

'Not properly, not completely, no.'

'The lack could be to do with not finding the right person yet,' she suggested.

He shrugged. 'Or it could be to do with how often that perfection comes. Perhaps not to all of us.'

'What if you and I don't achieve it?' she asked, and discovered her heart beating rapidly because that was tantamount to saying she would go to bed with him. Yet this honesty from Joe Jordan had broken through her defences more than anything else could have, she realised.

'We'll be a little older and a little wiser,' he said gently. 'And perhaps there will be a corner of your heart for a bloke who wanted you desperately but—fell down in other areas.'

'I never thought I would go to bed with a man I wasn't sure about, Joe, but at this moment, and although it may not last, you have a corner of my heart. Come.'

And she led him out of the kitchen.

His bedroom had the luxury of a double bed beneath an elegant fitted beige and white patterned spread

It also had a lovely old cedar wardrobe with brass handles, its doors lined with oval mirrors, a beige wall-to-wall carpet and white curtains tied back with ties made from the bedspread material. The walls were painted a soft ochre, two white marble lamps stood on the bedside tables and there was a comfortable russet velvet-covered armchair. It was the only room in the house that looked as if someone had decorated it to a plan and created a harmonious effect.

Lydia stopped on the threshold, she'd never seen this room before, and turned to him with a raised eyebrow.

'We decided to get the house redecorated a couple of years ago but we never got beyond this bedroom and Sarah and Rolf's.'

'It's nice.' She was still holding his hand, but she dropped it and went into the room to stroke the lovely lines of the cedar wardrobe.

'I'm glad you approve,' he murmured, looming up behind her so they were both reflected in the mirrors, 'but I hope it hasn't deflected us in any way.'

Lydia paused, and experienced a trill of sensation running through her at the way he was looking down at her in the mirror. 'No,' she murmured, turning to face him. 'My mind is made up.'

His lips twisted, and this time he took her hand and raised it to his lips.

'Unless…' she hesitated '…I'm being too bossy?'

'Believe me, I couldn't approve more.'

She stared at him, suddenly wary. 'No, Joe, I mean, I know I *can* be, and—'

'I see there's only way to resolve this impasse, Lydia.' And he took her into his arms and started to kiss her.

From there on being bossy was the last thing on her mind. And the magic of what they did to each other was heightened by their reflection in the mirror. It created a new dimension for Lydia, to see herself in his arms, to see the colour fluctuating in her cheeks as well as feel it as he drew her blouse off and stared down at her grey velvet bra with roses etched into the soft, silky pile.

'I often wear it,' she said breathlessly.

'Which means you didn't put it on especially to drive me wild tonight?'

'No, I didn't know—' She broke off and bit her lip, because it sounded as if she was defending herself. 'No,' she amended. 'But the briefs match.'

He laughed softly and put his hands on the waistband of her jeans. 'So Ms Kelso, veterinarian extraordinaire, has a secret passion for gorgeous undies?'

'She does,' she agreed.

'I hope she won't object to me taking them off?'

'Please do,' she murmured, with a smile trembling on her lips. 'But before you do, Ms Kelso also has a passion for equality. You were rather breathtaking without your shirt earlier.'

He took his hands from her body and stripped the top of his tracksuit off speedily. 'How's that?'

She grinned and laid her cheek against his chest, then started to laugh.

'That's not very kind,' he objected.

'I'm not laughing at you like this. I'm thinking of how your voice changed when you stepped under the tank shower.'

'Ah. I was hoping you hadn't heard that!'

She lifted her head and her eyes were dancing. But something else came to them as he slid his hands around her back and undid her bra.

It dropped with a whisper to the carpet, and although he made no move to touch them his eyes were on her breasts, small, close mounds that lay sleekly on her slender torso, in perfect proportion with it and tipped with natural velvet.

Perhaps it was something in the intensity of his gaze, perhaps it was the cool night air, but those velvet tips flowered, and he drew in a suddenly uneven breath and covered each one with the palms of his hands.

'OK?' she asked barely audibly.

'Exquisite. May I see the briefs?'

She could only nod.

And, still in front of the mirror, they helped each other to undress.

The briefs caused a smile to touch his mouth, but they soon met the same fate as her bra, and then they were glorying in being in each other's arms with no impediment between them.

There was also a tempo building up between them of rhythmic desire as they touched each other, fitted into each other and savoured the different textures of their skin, the different shapes and lines of their bodies. And finally, with her arms around his neck, he cupped her hips and lifted her, as she wound her legs around him, and carried her to bed.

The tempo became like a drumbeat as she lay beneath him, so skilled was he, so patient at times, gentle and funny, yet never letting her doubt for a moment that he wanted her desperately. And her reintroduction to sex after nearly six years of chastity came in waves of sheer desire she could only marvel at and savour with extreme pleasure, until the final peak of pleasure claimed them both.

Then he wrapped her in his arms, cocooned them in blankets, and stroked her hair until she fell asleep.

Dawn was just rimming the horizon when she woke, to find him dressed and sitting beside her on the bed.

She stretched luxuriously, then pulled the blankets up under her arms and said, 'Good morning. You didn't have to wait to go to work until I woke.'

'Yes, I did,' he replied. 'I'm not going to work just yet.'

Unaware that her skin, in the lamplight, was like ivory satin, and her eyes as blue as sapphires, she looked her fill of him for a long moment, then reached for his hand and kissed the knuckles. 'Thanks,' she said huskily.

'No thanks are due,' he said softly. 'It was mutual.' But he held her gaze compellingly.

Aware, immediately, of what he was asking her—had it existed in its own right?—she said, with complete honesty, 'Yes.'

Something flickered in the hazel depths of his eyes that she thought might have been relief, but it was gone as he said, 'Then I've had rather a good idea. I got up about an hour ago and made some preparations. All you have to do is get dressed.'

'What for?'

'Ah, I know what you mean.' His gaze skimmed down her figure beneath the blankets and her bare shoulders above them. 'Well, we could do that instead, but—'

Her fingers tightened on his briefly. 'That wasn't what I meant, Mr Jordan. Should I get dressed to go to work or stay at home is what I meant!'

He grinned. 'I knew that. Just couldn't help testing you out. Uh—going out, but not to work. My horse and Billy are saddled up and tied to the garden fence, I thought a gallop to the waterfall as the sun comes up, and a swim...' He stopped quizzically as Lydia drew in a breath. 'Like the idea?'

She sat up, uncaring of the blanket slipping down to her waist. 'You're a genius, Joe Jordan!'

It was a magical gallop through a world waking up to a new day.

At one stage they flushed out two emus with their striped chicks, the adults keeping pace with them for a short while before turning back to the chicks.

Lydia tore off her hat and yodelled with sheer exhilaration beneath a dome of blue streaked with lemon and apricot as Billy flew, in his sure-footed way, across the sandy-pink, sage-green dotted earth. The air was chilly but as clear as glass, so every breath hung on it and the tip of her nose was freezing. Then the lemon and apricot faded from the sky and the sun appeared over the edge of the earth—or so it seemed to her—and tiny droplets of dew on low bushes and bare branches radiated the light, and spider webs trapped moisture on every filament so that they looked like snowflakes.

They slowed their horses to a walk eventually, as they made their way down to the water holes, and there was another marvel to greet them. Flocks of white, sulphur-crested cockatoos and pink and grey galahs, rising in squawking surprise—so many of them she could only gasp in wonderment.

'They weren't here last time!' she exclaimed as she slid off Billy, looped the reins over his head and patted his sweating neck appreciatively.

'We probably scared them away, and we did have a fire. There was also more water in other places,' Joe remarked, and stripped off his gloves.

He looked, she thought, the consummate bushman in his flat-brimmed hat and distinctively caped Driza-Bone oilskin coat, over a red and white checked flannel shirt, jeans and boots.

She said, involuntarily, 'You look like *The Man From Snowy River*.'

He grinned. 'This ain't much of a river, ma'am, and a long way from Kosciusko, but I can guarantee it'll be snowy!'

She shivered inside her yellow thermal jacket, and laughed. Then she watched him untie his saddle rolls, and did the same to those that were attached to her saddle.

When everything was laid out, she murmured, 'You were busy, Joe, while I was fast asleep.' And shook her head again in wonderment. Because laid out on the sandy bank were the billy and tripod, mugs, plates, milk, tea and sugar, honey and butter and, the *coup de grâce*, a round golden damper. There were also a couple of nets of lucerne hay for the horses.

'I cheated a bit,' he said modestly. 'I cooked the

damper in the stove at the home; it should be done in the coals of a camp oven.'

'I'm not complaining. And we can keep it warm in the coals.'

'Good thinking,' he said gravely. 'Shall we water our horses, then I'll make a fire, start the billy and we can decide whether to swim first—or afterwards?'

'I'll look after the horses; you can concentrate on the fire.'

'You really are a woman after my own heart, Lydia!'

She didn't reply as she led both horses down to the pool, but she shot him a laughing little look.

'We're crazy!' she said later as they stood beside the same pool half undressed—they were both stripped to their shirts and underpants. 'I'm blue with cold.' The fire was going and the horses, tied to trees, were munching their lucerne contentedly.

'Just think how nice it will be when we come out and sit around the fire—and there is another factor to consider.'

'I can't think of one!'

'Well, freezing water is renowned for freezing certain ambitions of the masculine variety, so you'll be quite safe from me, in certain respects, for a time. I can't specify how long, but—'

'Oh, well,' she broke in, 'when you put it like that I have little choice!' And, taking a deep breath, she pulled off the rest of her clothes and plunged in. He followed suit.

'Not only crazy, stark, staring *bonkers*,' she spluttered about five minutes later. 'Why didn't you tell me there were crocodiles?'

They were back on the bank and Joe was rubbing her down vigorously with a rough towel. He had pulled his jeans on but she, as yet, wore nothing.

'I thought you knew; you mentioned them the first time we swam—'

'Yes, but I didn't expect to come face to face with one!'

'Lydia, they're Johnson River crocs, they don't attack people, we were quite safe. Mind you, I got a bit of a surprise myself.'

Her teeth chattered as she said with extreme frustration, 'But I got such an awful fright—I could have drowned!'

'Here.' He dropped the towel and picked up her undies. She grabbed them and stepped into her briefs and clasped her bra on, a different one, lacy and white with a navy blue satin bow that matched her briefs.

'That's the other thing! Being naked didn't help!' she told him tartly.

'I'm sure it didn't,' he murmured soothingly, and helped her to put on her thin white woollen pullover. 'Not that a swimming costume provides much of a deterrent for a crocodile with serious man-eating on his mind,' he added.

She shot him a withering look, but he merely provided himself placidly as something to hang on to as she hopped into her jeans, one leg at a time, and wriggled vigorously to eliminate the resistance her cold skin was offering to the denim. He also helped her, gravely, to give them a final tug up.

'You give new meaning to being poured into a pair of jeans, Lydia,' he offered respectfully.

She let go of him suddenly. 'That's only because I'm still damp!' she retorted arctically as she pulled on her yellow jacket and sat down abruptly to reach for her socks and boots.

She was still brooding on the sheer, heart-stopping terror of coming face to face with a crocodile—admittedly a startled one. All the same, she'd been unable to move a muscle, and had started to sink before Joe had grabbed her and, with the lifesaving technique that she'd experienced before, towed her to the bank whilst the creature had swum away in the other direction and disappeared into the next pool.

But with her boots zipped up, she crossed her legs and turned her attention to Joe Jordan.

He now had his shirt on as well as his jeans, and with a wry little glance at her he came to sit down opposite her, also cross-legged, so that their knees touched, and started to button up the shirt.

Lydia maintained her disapproval for a good minute as they stared into each other's eyes, until she looked down first and realised he'd got his buttons crooked.

'Let me,' she murmured, and he surrendered them to her, saying nothing, although his gaze was quizzical as it rested on her bent head.

When she'd finished, she looked up into his eyes again, austerely, but she also straightened his collar with one hand then slipped her hand round the back of his neck. And as their foreheads touched, she said on a gurgle of laughter, 'I feel such a fool!'

They laughed together until she was almost crying. Then she pulled a hanky from her pocket to wipe her eyes and nose, and he said, 'That's my girl.'

'But if you had a romantic, naked tryst beneath the waterfall in mind, Joe, I couldn't have ruined it more effectively.'

'That water was too cold to be romantic, and that croc

had other ideas; it wasn't one of my better plans,' he admitted ruefully.

'It was a lovely one,' Lydia contradicted. 'I'll cherish the ride, the sunrise, even the croc and half freezing.' She looked around and it was plain to see the magic that the spot, and the morning, was reawakening in her.

'And I'll be content with that—for the time being,' he murmured.

She waited until he'd retrieved the damper, wrapped in foil, from the coals, and poured the tea from the billy, before she said, 'About last night.'

He paused to look at her briefly, then went on buttering the damper he'd sliced.

'Can I just make some observations as they come to mind?' she asked with a faintly puzzled frown.

'If you want to.'

She studied him for a long moment. 'Don't you think it should be talked about, Joe?'

He shrugged. 'It could be difficult to put into words.'

'I'm entirely in agreement, about some of it. But if you're worried I'm going to put you through a "Was I any good?" kind of routine, I'm not.'

'You were. You reminded me of the *Song of Solomon*.'

'Oh, Joe,' she whispered, 'you don't have to say that.'

He handed her a slice of damper dripping with butter and honey on a tin plate, and for an instant his hazel gaze held hers and it was completely serious.

So much so that she was shaken to the core, and she'd finished her damper and tea before she came out of her reverie. Nor did he intrude on her thoughts, but when she did come out of it, he raised an enquiring eyebrow at her.

She shook her head. 'No, you're right; I can't put anything into words.'

He smiled slightly and held out his hand to her. She took it and he drew her to her feet, then slid his arms around her beneath her open jacket. And for at least five minutes he demonstrated how unnecessary words were between them.

She was breathless, flushed and had stars in her eyes when they stopped kissing each other passionately, causing him to tell her that she was a sight for sore eyes.

'Oh, dear,' she said decorously.

He grinned and reached for his coat to shrug it on. 'What does that mean?'

'I've got the feeling I actually look all starstruck and girlish.'

He took her in his arms again and rested his forehead on hers. 'Not exactly like the Ms Kelso who arrived on Katerina, or bearded me in Balmain, no,' he said barely audibly.

Her lips trembled, but she said gravely, 'Quite a dragon she must have appeared to you.'

He considered. 'All the same that was when I first experienced the desire to see you without your clothes. As I mentioned so disastrously when we remet.'

'Your choice of words did leave a lot to be desired,' she agreed. 'But I have to admit you were the first man to intrigue me for a long time.'

He kissed her mouth lightly. 'I'm glad. Should we head home?'

'Let's.'

They rode home more sedately and via a different route, stopping once on a rise at a boundary fence where they could see the Victoria River as it flowed in a series of curves towards some distant mountains, now browsing in golden sunlight, on its journey to the sea and the Joseph Bonaparte Gulf.

And Joe told her a bit about Augustus Gregory who, in 1855 and 1886, had discovered the vast grazing lands of the Victoria River Basin as well as the rugged, virtually inaccessible country around it.

Lydia sat on her horse, drinking it all in, and was unaware that he was watching her rather intently as her expression radiated her delight in the vast Top End panorama.

They were to have three more days on their own.

Sarah rang to say that she and Rolf were still trying to talk things through. Joe put the phone down and stared into the distance thoughtfully; the call had come in just after they'd got back to the homestead from their ride and swim.

'How does she sound?' Lydia asked.

'Distracted. Jumpy. Very tense,' he replied.

'Would it help if you were there with her?'

'I don't think so. I'm a large part of Rolf's problem, so to speak.' He shrugged. 'No, I think this has to be between them.'

Lydia went up to him and put her arms around his waist. 'I can see you suffering for her, though, and I know what it's like.'

He looked into her eyes and his lips twisted. 'Fate seems to have decreed that you and I bear the responsibility of our sisters.'

She touched his cheek with her fingertips. 'I'd love to be able to help.'

He caught her hand and kissed her fingers.

'I mean, I know I can't actually help with Sarah and

Rolf,' she continued after a moment. 'But with the other dislocation of your life. It has to be a huge step for you, giving up your cartooning to come back to Katerina, even although you love it.'

'I didn't think you approved of my cartooning,' he said with a fleeting smile.

'I was determined not to approve of anything to do with Joe Jordan at the time,' she said wryly. 'Obviously you've won me over to a certain extent since then.'

His eyebrows shot up. 'Only to a certain extent?'

She maintained a calm expression, although their proximity was creating havoc with her senses. They'd shed their jackets and she was able to feel the warmth of his body against hers, inhale the heady scent of a mixture of sweat after their ride back and strength. She wondered as she stood against him how it could be described as strength, but that was how it struck her; that was the difference between the perfume of her skin and his, and that was what made it so heady and exciting.

She swallowed suddenly, remembering his question, and was struck by the fact that although she'd been teasing him she was in fact gloriously if not foolishly won over.

'To a large extent, then,' she said airily, still trying to keep it light.

He looked amused. He said, however, 'Well, this evening I have to pound out a two-thousand-word article for the paper. You might like to give me your assessment of it.'

'I'd love to,' she responded, although looking genuinely surprised.

'Good. But now I have to do some work, much as I'd love to—do something else with you.'

It was her turn to look amused. 'Can I come? Is there anything for me to do?'

'You may, with pleasure,' he responded. 'Like to do a bit of mustering from the chopper?'

'I'd love to! But who…are you flying it?'

He nodded. 'Pete's had to go into Timber Creek to pick up a part for the grader. And this next paddock has some rough country in it.'

'But I didn't know you flew!'

'I may have mentioned before that I was modesty personified?'

She looked into his wicked hazel eyes and said a little helplessly, 'Nobody else mentioned it either.'

'Probably didn't cross their minds. We employ Pete because Rolf doesn't fly, and although a lot of stations use contract helicopter mustering, it's handy to have your own, if you can fly one.'

'I see. Don't they cost a small fortune? And you also have a plane.'

He grinned. 'I picked both of them up secondhand, Ms Kelso, and, together with Pete, renovated them.'

She shook her head. 'There's no end to you, Mr Jordan!'

'In that case—come fly with me, Lydia!'

She did.

So she spent the next few hours diving down ravines and up gullies, clinging on and shutting her eyes at times, as they chased cattle out on to the plain into the waiting arms of the mustering team. The noise was tremendous, despite her earphones, but Joe's cool daring and complete understanding of the limitations of his machine were wildly impressive.

'That was tremendously exciting but I'm exhausted!' she confessed when they returned to the homestead after dark. 'I feel as if I've been pounded and battered and I've got a headache.' She grimaced. 'How feeble!'

He grinned down at her. 'Not feeble at all. It takes a bit of getting used to. Why don't you soak in a hot bath and I'll make us a drink? You deserve it.'

She sighed. 'That sounds wonderful, but I only have a shower in my bathroom.'

'Lydia.' He caught her wrist as she went to go past him. 'Use mine. It's got a proper full-length bath.'

'Well—may I?' But she sounded suddenly hesitant.

He released her wrist and traced the outline of her mouth. 'Of course. Because we are going to use my bedroom tonight, aren't we?'

She distinctly felt herself go weak inside, and could only nod.

She didn't soak for long, although she did lie back and apply a hot facecloth to her brow for about five minutes, which seemed to cure her headache. As she got out of the bath, Joe came in.

He pulled a towel from the rail and murmured, 'You have no idea what will-power I exerted this morning when I dried you off, Lydia.'

Her lips parted as she stood before him, naked and dripping. 'I…I mean, I assumed…' she stammered like an inarticulate girl, and couldn't go on.

Tiny lines crinkled beside his eyes as he smiled wryly. 'You mean you were so mad at me you failed to notice that, freezing water and a Johnson River croc notwith-standing, I was seriously stricken with desire for you?' he teased.

'Well, yes,' she confessed. 'But you also told me what

the effect of the water was likely to be!' She breathed in deeply as he started to towel her.

'Just think…' he lifted her arm to dry her side '..how powerful your attraction must be, then.'

She closed her eyes, because all she could think of was the effect his gentle yet thorough towelling was having on her. Then she said softly, although with her eyes still closed, 'Hang on.'

His hands stilled where they just happened to be, cupping her hips through the towel. 'Lydia?'

She lifted her lashes at last and there was a spark of devilry in the deep blue of her eyes, as well as desire. 'I'd just like to assess how powerful it is now.'

'I'll tell you,' he replied plaintively. 'If you don't take me to bed pretty soon, I shall be lost.'

'You started this,' she reminded him.

He gazed down at her quizzically. 'Ah, but only you can complete it.'

Her lips curved. 'All the same, I'd much rather you took me to bed, Joe.'

'Why?'

She shrugged, and he dropped the towel and moved his hands round to her breasts. He also said, 'Do that again.'

'What? Shrug?'

'Please.'

'No, Joe—'

'It's—breathtaking, the way they move, that's all,' he said seriously.

'Joe, I'm not going to stand here shrugging all—oh, all right! Come to bed, Joe Jordan!' She took his hand and led him out of the bathroom.

CHAPTER SEVEN

WHEN they got up, Lydia donned her pyjamas and dressing gown and said she'd make them bacon and eggs, if that was all right with him.

'Mmm, sounds perfect.' But he put his arms around her.

He'd pulled on a tracksuit, and while she'd kept her hair dry as they'd showered together his was still damp, and standing up in spikes from the towelling he'd given it. She resisted the urge to tame them by combing her fingers through his hair, then gave way to it, causing him to smile gravely.

'How was that?' he asked.

The corners of her mouth dimpled. 'I thought we weren't supposed to talk about it.'

He considered. 'That was this morning. It seems to be different this evening, but I did—'

She put her fingers to his lips. 'I know, you did make the most wonderful reference to it. How was it tonight?' She paused and her mind roamed back to the pleasure he'd brought her, the soaring climax so that her spirit as well as her body had been transported to a peak of perfection... 'It was exquisite,' she said huskily, and trembled suddenly in his arms.

He kissed her lightly and with extreme gentleness. 'I couldn't have said it better myself.'

'Why don't you go and exercise your way with words, then, while I do the cooking?' she suggested.

He laughed, and she caught her breath because there

was something so alive and devastatingly attractive
about him it caught at her heart.

She not only cooked bacon and eggs, she fried tomatoes
and made a lot of chips. She set it all out on a warming
trolley, complete with a bottle of tomato sauce, and
wheeled it, with a flask of coffee, into his study.

He looked up from his computer and held out his hand
to her.

'How's it going?'

'Nearly done. Wow! Chips and tomato sauce. I must
have been doing some things right lately.' He drew her
down on to his lap.

'As you very well know, Mr Jordan,' she murmured,
with her head resting comfortably on his shoulder, 'I like
your study. I liked your other study, as a matter of fact.
I even...' She paused.

'Go on,' he invited.

'No, nothing. Well,' she said at his quizzical expression, 'you might get a swollen head, so I won't say it.
Shall we eat?'

He gazed at her enigmatically, giving her to understand, by making no movement and keeping his arms
around her, that she wasn't going to get away with being
mysterious.

She clicked her tongue with humorous frustration, but
secretly she had other reasons for changing tack and not
going on to say that she'd very much liked his Balmain
house, even to the extent of wanting one like it herself.
In case he realised just how far overboard she'd gone?
she asked herself.

'Lydia?'

She came out of her thoughts with a little jerk.

'Uh…Joe, it may not exactly be a gourmet meal, but we shouldn't waste it.'

'I'll make a bargain with you, then. We'll eat now if you promise to tell me what you were going to say over coffee.'

'That's blackmail,' she protested.

'I have a further string to my bow, although I'd hesitate to use it,' he drawled.

'Such as?' she enquired dangerously.

'Well, I know you've overpowered me a couple of times, but in the normal course of events, and fully prepared, I'm stronger than you are, so…' He shrugged.

'Joe Jordan, put me down.'

He grinned satanically.

'I mean let me go!' she commanded.

'Only if you promise.'

'This is childish!'

'I'm a big kid at heart; look how I like my chips,' he murmured.

She looked into his eyes instead, which was a mistake, because there was so much laughter in them once again she went breathless at the impact of him. 'All right, Tarzan,' she said unsteadily, 'I'll promise—to think about it.'

'That's not—'

'Joe!'

'Yes, ma'am! Just doing it, ma'am.' He released her.

'Now you've made me feel like a schoolmistress.'

He lifted her to her feet and stood up himself, kissed her, and took her hand to lead her towards the trolley. 'As a mistress you're sensational, even when you comb my hair for me and do up my buttons. I'm starving,' he continued as her lips parted. 'Thank you so much for providing this feast.' And he drew up two stools and started to unload the trolley on to a table.

Predictably, Lydia subsided, then started to smile, and finally burst out laughing. She said, 'I've got the feeling you could charm a block of wood.'

He smothered his chips with tomato sauce and looked at her ruefully. 'So long as you don't hold it against me.'

In the event she didn't have to tell him anything, nor did she get to read his article, because before they'd had a chance to drink their coffee a call came through from the head ringer out on the plain. The mob that Lydia and Joe had mustered by chopper had been settled for the night, preparatory to moving them to the portable yards tomorrow for drafting. But one of the ringers keeping watch had been thrown from his horse when it had been startled by a snake and had broken his leg: a nasty compound fracture, apparently, that would require the attention of the Flying Doctor.

He'd also hit his head and didn't seem to know where he was.

Before Lydia's eyes, Joe went from laid-back, teasing and relaxed to ice-cool and very much in command.

There were a couple of supply vehicles at the scene, fortunately, and one of them was bringing the ringer in. So the main concern was to get the airstrip lit so the Flying Doctor could land, and provide palliative care until he arrived.

'I can help there,' Lydia said. 'I know I'm not a doctor, but—'

'Good,' Joe interrupted briefly. 'Thanks.' Then, as his gaze rested on her, it softened. 'I'm sorry. You were already exhausted—'

'It doesn't matter. I'm fine. Let's go.'

*   *   *

By sunrise the next morning she fell into bed, her own bed, and slept for six hours. During the dark hours of the night she'd not only helped to build fires and prime lanterns to light the strip, but she'd monitored the ringer's condition and been patched through to the doctor via satellite telephone, so she'd been able to keep him stabilised. The Flying Doctor had just commenced the return trip to Darwin.

Joe had gone back to the muster. She'd offered, but had been told gently but firmly to go to bed.

She swam up from deep layers of sleep just before lunchtime, stretched, and found her gaze dwelling on Brad's picture on the dressing table. Something like a shaft of pain pierced her heart, because it had been a couple of days since she'd thought of him, and not only that, she'd given herself to another man under the weight of an attraction so strong it had driven him from her mind.

Or had it? she asked herself as she sat up and reached for the silver-framed photo. Could it be that Joe and Brad would always occupy different parts of her heart? Could it be a blessing of Brad's that she could now go forward to love again because she was able to draw on the things he'd taught her and shared with her?

She blinked a couple of times, then held his image to her heart for a long moment, before putting it back on the dressing table.

Although, of course, she mused, neither she nor Joe had discussed being in love with each other, or where it would lead. But perhaps this release she felt, to go forward with Brad's blessing, would…what? she wondered. It had to make it easier for her, if nothing else. Unless she should still be very wary about falling in love so quickly. But that was how it had happened for her *with*

Brad. The difference being, though, she thought, with an odd little tremor running through her, she and Brad had both been of one mind, whereas Joe...

'Is still something of an enigma.' She said it out aloud and frowned as she remembered his disinclination to talk about it. And there was something else, she realised, that she couldn't quite put her finger on, except to think *was* he more manageable than she'd expected? She shook her head immediately, because it wasn't that, but...

Finally she gave up and got up. Although as she showered she made one decision. She would just go with the flow for the time being.

It was in this spirit, the following evening, that she barred Joe from the kitchen and prepared a special meal: a delicate zucchini soup, veal with mushrooms in a cream sauce, and *crêpes Suzette* to finish. She set the rarely used table in the main dining room with Sarah's best linen, found some candles, put on a heater and retired to her room.

Half an hour later she emerged, lit the candles and dished up the soup, calling him from his study. Although they'd spent the day together it had always been amongst others, and the night before had seen Joe so tired they'd slept together but 'most chastely', as he'd put it with a wicked little grin.

He came as soon as she called, but paused on the threshold, taking in the candles, the bottle of wine, the soft music in the background, the warm room, and her. 'You should have warned me,' he said at last, and looked down at his jeans and navy jumper.

Lydia moved forward in her black silk georgette dress, and took his hand. 'I just felt this dress...' she smoothed it '...didn't get to—didn't *quite* get to realise its full potential the last time I wore it,' she murmured.

He smiled faintly, his gaze examining her discreet make-up and shining loose hair.

'Besides which,' she continued softly, 'Sarah told me you have to make your own entertainment in this part of the world, so I thought I would not only cook you a special dinner, I'd dress up for you.'

'I see,' he said at last. 'I can only approve.'

'I'm glad,' she murmured gravely, and led him to the table.

'You wouldn't also be laughing at me?' he enquired.

'Why would I do that?'

'Because I may have looked completely bowled over?'

'You did look satisfyingly stunned,' she conceded.

'You do know what's going to happen after dinner, Lydia? Assuming I can wait that long,' he said.

They were standing very close and she could see the shadows on his jaw, those little lines beside his eyes and what was lurking in their hazel depths: a preoccupation and fascination with her that caused her to breathe unsteadily.

'Oh, yes,' she said huskily, and touched those shadows, feeling the roughness of his skin with her fingertips 'Oh, yes, Joe. And I can only approve...'

They made love later with an intensity that shouldn't have surprised her, because all through her special meal, or as far as they'd got, the tension had grown—the tension of trying to be good company and make conversation, of according her food the respect it deserved—when really the last thing either of them had wanted to be doing was eating and talking...

Nor had they got to the dessert stage, because before she'd finished her veal she'd put her napkin on the table and looked across at him rather helplessly.

He'd risen, come round to her and drawn her to her feet, then clasped both her hands in his between them, level with her breasts. 'Would I be terribly uncouth if I also declined dessert?' he'd murmured, his eyelids half lowered, his voice deep and quiet.

'Yes. I mean, no... I mean, I was going to agree that...dessert could wait. That's what I meant,' she'd said lamely.

His lips had twisted. 'Then it seems we're of one mind.'

'Yes...' She hadn't been able to think of a single thing to add, had barely been able to breathe, as her pulses leapt and a flame of desire swept through her. And this time it had been he who led her to his bedroom.

All the same, he'd started slowly. He'd kissed her thoroughly first, then undone her lovely dress so that it had slithered down her thighs with a silken hush. Her underwear was black lace tonight, and the removing of it had involved touching her intimately. She hadn't helped, powerless, she'd discovered, other than to accept being undressed and thrill to the sensations he'd been inflicting on her.

It had struck her once, dimly, that if she'd set the scene for this seduction, he was carrying it through in a way that was killing her slowly, with love and a yearning of the most physical kind.

She'd also felt as if she should make a stand of some kind, play some part, but when she'd been free of her clothes, and he'd dispensed quickly with his, she had still been standing in the middle of the floor, with her arms at her sides, unable to move because she'd never felt more slender, or vulnerable suddenly, at the power of the attraction of his tall, sleek and strong body, and the way he handled hers.

Then he had come to her, and, after one brief, searching look into her stunned eyes, said very quietly as he touched her mouth gently, 'Don't look like that; it's mutual.'

That had been when it became not only mutual but extremely urgent as they'd claimed each other with an intensity that hadn't allowed them to reach the bed.

Hours later, after they'd made love again, but much more decorously, on the bed, she stirred and laid her cheek on his chest. He stroked her hair. 'All right?'

'Mmm...'

'Want to talk?'

'What about?' she murmured.

He paused, slipping strand after strand of hair through his fingers. 'How well we do some things on our feet?'

A smile curved her lips. 'I knew you'd make some reference to that, Joe.'

'Did you, now? In point of fact, that's the first time it's happened that way for me.'

'In point of fact, me too, and I feel...' it was her turn to pause '...slightly embarrassed about it.'

'I can't agree there.' His fingers drifted down her cheek to her chin, which he tilted so he could see her eyes. 'It was marvellous. It was spontaneous combustion, you might say.'

'It was certainly that.'

'So I don't see why there should be any regrets, but if you prefer I shall desist from the upright position in future.'

She blinked at him. 'You were...' She stopped.

'Lydia, you still have one other thing you started to say then refused to enlighten me about, and it's unlikely that anyone is going to fall off their horse and fracture their leg again so soon.'

'Is that a threat, Joe? Anyway, I...I thought you'd forgotten.'

'Not at all, on both counts.'

'So why make the point?'

'Because I could keep you in bed with me for days. But would you see that as a threat? Or a penance?'

She leant up on one elbow and observed him dryly. 'Yes. Well, not a penance exactly...'

'Not exactly?' he teased.

'Damn. I should never get into an argument with you, Joe—you know what I mean!'

'I do now, and if you'll just tell me what you were going to say earlier, I'll get up and make us a midnight snack.'

'I was going to say you were the one who initiated the spontaneous combustion!'

'Ah, I'm not so sure about that. Your black dress is actually renowned for the effect it has on me.'

Lydia stared at him, then suddenly dissolved into laughter. 'I didn't expect quite such an effect, though.'

He kissed her hair and hugged her. 'Why was that so hard to say?'

'I don't know,' she murmured, after some thought. 'Did you say something about a midnight snack?'

'Just going.'

She lay in his bed and could hear him in the kitchen, talking to Meg and producing the snack. And she wondered why it had been so hard to say, and what she'd *really* been trying to say anyway? But all she could define was that it seemed to be linked with something on her mind to do with Joe Jordan that refused to make itself clear to her, something worrying.

She sighed, pulled the blankets up to her chin and contemplated the fact that she felt wrecked in the most wonderful way, so it was an odd time to be having doubts about the man who had achieved this—unless it was to do with just how good he was at it?

She sat up abruptly as things suddenly slid more into focus for her. Had she been subconsciously congratulating herself on handling things between them to her satisfaction and at her pace? Had she secretly liked to think he was quite manageable when in fact he'd only been allowing her to think it?

But why, she asked herself, did this occur to her now? What had unlocked this growing conviction that she'd managed nothing, but had been led with great subtlety and charm along a path that she wouldn't have had a hope in hell of resisting anyway? Was it the way she'd melted tonight and seemed to lose all will? So that her planned seduction after a good meal, intelligent conversation, music, candles and all the trimmings had been overpowered by something she'd had no control over?

Was it the knowledge now that he was irresistible and she was no better at being immune from him than Daisy had been? In fact, had she been lured into being as notoriously generous as her sister could be on very few grounds for anything permanent likely to develop from it?

She swallowed, and remembered something he'd said two nights ago, when she'd told him she suspected he could charm a block of wood—*So long as you don't hold it against me.*

'Lydia?'

She looked up, startled, because she hadn't heard him come in, and he was standing beside the bed with a tray in his hands. 'Oh. That...that looks great.'

There were toasted cheese sandwiches and a pot of tea on the tray.

He put it down on the bedside table. 'What were you thinking about?'

She hesitated, and couldn't help wondering how he would prise it out of her if she refused to tell him. 'I was feeling lonely, I guess,' she said a little sadly, which was true, but not quite as he might imagine.

He sat down on the side of the bed and kissed her forehead. 'It was lonely out in the kitchen.'

'At least you had Meg,' she murmured.

'You know how I adore Meg, but it's not the same thing at all. May I come back in?'

'Joe...of course!' But it had not been what she was going to say. Joe, you don't fool me any more, she'd been going to say. You've got me literally eating out of your hand, but I'm no longer the only one who didn't know it...

'I thought you might have been having second thoughts.'

They'd eaten their sandwiches, drunk their tea, and laughingly remade the bed, getting rid of the crumbs. They were now lying in the dark, she with her head on his shoulder but wide awake.

'I'm probably a bit dazed,' she said at last.

'Lydia—'

'And wondering whether I'm a control freak.'

She felt his jolt of laughter. 'Because your beautiful dinner, *et al*, didn't go quite according to plan?'

She nodded gratefully, because he'd understood immediately—although that was only half of it, and the least important part of it.

'We could do it again tomorrow night. I promise to behave myself.'

'I don't think so, Joe.'

'How would it be if we slept on it and made any momentous decisions to do with it tomorrow?'

'We do...we do need to talk,' she said, a little unsteadily. Then added hastily, 'But you're right. Tomorrow.'

He kissed her hair. 'I don't mind talking now. But I thought you might be a little highly strung at the moment. So, turn over, and I'll see what I can do about it.'

She hesitated, uncomfortably aware that he'd read her state of mind accurately and feeling foolish in consequence. Then she did as she was bid and he started to stroke her back gently.

And, quite helpless beneath the rhythm of his hand, she felt herself softening and relaxing, even starting to feel sleepy. 'I thought I was the one with the magic hands,' she murmured drowsily.

'You are, but this is a pleasure compared to a chore.'

She fell asleep with a smile on her lips.

There was a note on the pillow when she woke to say that he was down at the main yards to take delivery of a breeding bull they'd purchased, and also that Sarah had rung and Pete, who'd been in Darwin to pick up supplies, was bringing her home to Katerina. They'd be back later in the morning. It finished with a query— would she like to come down and inspect the new bull?

Lydia brushed her hair out of her eyes, glanced at the bedside clock, then scrambled out of bed. It was already nine-thirty and she'd slept through not only Joe leaving but the phone ringing; she'd slept on despite the remains of a meal and an untidy kitchen to deal with, but also having taken up residence in Joe's bedroom, and now Sarah was due home shortly, with all the attendant unhappiness that might bring.

And he thought she had time to go down and see a bull?

She smiled briefly as she headed for the shower, amused at herself mostly, and her housewifely concerns, when she had far larger issues hanging over her head, but nothing seemed to dent her determination to hand Sarah's house back to her spick and span. Not even the question on her mind of whether Joe Jordan was standing on the outside of *their* relationship and feeling a lack…

Because she'd succumbed like every other woman he'd known? Had he been hoping, when he'd allowed her to think she was calling the tune, that she'd call a different tune? Was that what he'd meant—Don't hold it against me when you find out you're no different from the others?

It was quite by accident that she heard Sarah before she saw her.

Pete flew over the homestead as usual, but there was no vehicle up at the house so Lydia assumed Joe would pick Sarah up from the airstrip. And she suddenly decided she would give them some time on their own before she intruded, so she put on her hat and went for a walk beyond the garden environs.

As she walked through the bush she pondered the new thoughts that had come to her as she'd showered. Was that why they'd neither of them simply said last night—

I love you? He, because it hadn't happened; she, because of a fear of what she would hear if she said it?

Hear that they needed more time before they made any decisions. Sensible, of course, she told herself, particularly in light of her new understanding that she was virtually like putty in his hands, but...

She was coming back and was just on the other side of the garden fence behind a stand of bushes when Sarah's clear voice and good enunciation wafted on the still, hot air, and she realised Sarah and her brother must be walking in the garden. To talk privately, perhaps, thinking Lydia was in the house?

She froze, then heard Sarah say, 'Joe, if you and Lydia were to make a go of it, that would be perfect! I needn't feel guilty about leaving you alone here; it's about time you settled down anyway, and she's so right for this place.'

'Beloved,' Lydia heard Joe drawl, 'those are not reasons to marry, much as I would like to accommodate you, and, to a lesser extent, Rolf.'

'But you have—I mean you and she have—got together, haven't you?'

'What makes you think that?' Joe sounded abrupt.

'Pete,' Sarah replied. 'He reckons it's happened.'

Lydia flinched as Joe swore. Then he said, with a clear warning in his voice, 'Sarah, what has happened between me and Lydia is our own business entirely. Don't trample about on it!'

'All right! But you can't deny if you're going to run Katerina you need a wife, and you need someone like Lydia. And Joe,' Sarah said firmly, 'love and all the rest of it may not be all it's cracked up to appear. Far better to have someone sensible by your side and let it grow.'

'Are you talking from your own experience?' Joe enquired cynically.

'Yes. What I love about Rolf now are not the same things I thought I saw in him when I was so madly attracted I couldn't think straight. I've been lucky,' she added soberly. 'I've got another chance. You know what your problem is? You're too darned independent.'

'Do you think marriage will solve that?'

They must have moved away, because Lydia didn't hear Sarah's reply, but Joe's question seemed to brand itself on her brain. She sat down on a rock and took off her hat to fan herself, not only because she was hot from the sun but because her heart was beating uncomfortably and another question posed itself to her.

Would she wait to discover whether Joe Jordan would offer to marry her because he needed a wife? Or would she acknowledge the truth of what Sarah had said, as Joe had, and get out before she broke her heart completely?

They were sitting in the garden, Joe and Sarah, on the other side of the house when Lydia ostensibly came back from her walk and managed to look suitably surprised as well as making her explanation of where she'd been.

Sarah got up immediately and hugged her enthusiastically. 'Sit down and have something to drink,' she said. 'I've got a lot to tell you!'

There was a tray on the grass with a pitcher of cold lime juice. Joe smiled at her and said, 'I won't embarrass you by kissing you without your permission, Lydia, but it seems the whole world knows we "got together", so you don't need to worry about covering anything up from Sarah. On the other hand, why not?' he murmured, and, taking her in his arms, kissed her lightly. 'You were a sleepyhead this morning,' he added, with his eyes wicked, teasing and warm all at the same time.

Then he released her and pulled up a chair for her, and she wasn't sure if she was furious with Joe Jordan or the opposite, but she did know that she was blushing furiously.

'Yes, well,' Sarah commented airily, 'I've been told not to trample about on this turn of events, so I won't, except to say—'

'Sarah.'

She turned to her brother and pulled a face at him. 'You won't always be there, Joe! But all right. Rolf and I have resolved our problems,' she said eagerly to Lydia. 'We're going to sell our shares to Joe, and Rolf has in mind a place in Queensland, out from Cooktown. It'll be a battle but instead of feeling like the meat in the sandwich at times, I shall—*we* shall have a common purpose from now on.'

'I don't know what to say,' Lydia conceded honestly. 'Except if it's what you truly want, I wish you all the success and happiness in the world.'

'Thanks. There's another piece of news I haven't even told Joe yet. They never could find out why I couldn't conceive, but I've seen a new specialist and he's of the opinion I don't need the *in vitro* program, I need, above all, to relax about it. I just didn't realise how tense I was, not only about a baby but seeing Rolf slipping away from me.'

Both Joe and Lydia leant forward and said, 'That's wonderful!' then grinned at each other and Sarah.

A little later Lydia got up to make lunch, protesting that she didn't need any help and they must have a lot to discuss. And she left them together after lunch, locked in critical business discussions by the sound of it, and took herself down finally to inspect the new bull.

'Would this be where I find the veterinarian, ma'am?'

Lydia looked up to see Joe standing at the door of the vet station, hat in hand.

'Perhaps.'

He came in. 'Then you're not the lady with the magic hands?'

A smile touched her mouth. 'I could be. But I also know a man with good hands.'

'Are you cross with me?'

'What makes you think that?' she asked.

'A certain sternness about you,' he replied. 'A certain air of preoccupation.'

'How long have you been watching me?'

'A minute or more. You were staring at the wall for all that time.'

Lydia glanced around the small room devoted to veterinary equipment that was built into the main shed. She'd come in with the idea of making an inventory of the sprays and drenches used for internal and external parasite control in cattle and horses, so she could pinpoint which stocks were low and perhaps suggest more updated alternatives. But her list lay on the table next to her pen and it was quite blank.

'You shouldn't watch people without their permission, Joe.'

'As in kissing them? Is that it?'

She looked up and found a certain irony in his gaze as it rested on her.

'No—I mean, it's sneaky—is that *what*?' she asked disjointedly.

'The reason for your mood?'

'There is no mood!' she denied.

He continued as if she hadn't spoken, 'Because I not only spilt the beans to Sarah but kissed you in front of her?'

'You could have consulted me first!' Lydia stared at him proudly.

'She already knew. The whole damn station knows. You may not have heard about the bush telegraph,' he said dryly, 'but even without it, for the last three days you've been going around like a woman in love, Lydia.'

She gasped.

'Not that there's anything wrong with that, it's been lovely to see, so why worry and get all uptight about Sarah knowing?'

She took several deep breaths. 'Because I can't say the same thing for you, Joe. I have, I've discovered, no idea whether you feel the same way.'

'No idea?' he said softly but lethally. 'Have you forgotten what happened to us only last night?'

'No. But I also haven't forgotten that we put off discussing it until today, and I happen to know that today may have brought a whole new complexion to things.' She stopped abruptly and bit her lip.

His eyes narrowed, and she flinched as she could see him making the connection—her walk, he and Sarah talking in the garden... 'You heard,' he said flatly.

'I...I didn't mean to,' she stammered. 'I went for a walk in the first place so you and Sarah could have a bit of time on your own, but I was just on the other side of those bushes...' She stopped helplessly.

'And you're now convinced I either need a wife, especially a sensible one like you, who's also right for Katerina, or I'm too independent to fall in love properly?'

'Joe, whatever and why ever...' she twisted her hands in obvious distress '...you are still something of an enigma to me. But it's worse. I thought...I thought I was handling this well—'

'Us?' He smiled briefly.

She nodded. 'That's what you let me think, though, isn't it?'

'Perhaps.'

Her eyes widened.

'Lydia,' he said, 'what should I have done? Trampled all over your memories of Brad or let you feel unthreatened and unpressured whilst I tried to be as manageable as I could?'

She licked her lips as several expressions chased through her eyes. 'Joe, that still doesn't tell me if you think we could be united, body and soul.'

He didn't move. 'Yes, I think we could,' he said quietly, 'but there's one thing I'm very afraid of. The pressures I may bring to bear whilst I get to grips with changing my life the way I'm about to.'

CHAPTER EIGHT

'JOE…' She stopped, supremely frustrated, as Pete rapped his knuckles on the door and stuck his head around it.

Joe himself said shortly, 'What is it now, Pete?'

'Uh…if this isn't a good time for you two,' Pete temporised, 'I can come back.'

But Lydia could clearly see the curiosity and amusement in the pilot's eyes. And she could feel herself getting hot at the thought of the whole station realising she was a woman in love and discussing it, perhaps laughing about the ups and downs of it, making predictions, even having bets?

She said, although in a strangled kind of way, 'Not at all, Pete. I was just about to go up to the house anyway.' And she walked out.

Joe made no attempt to follow her.

Nor did they have any further private communication until after dinner.

Over dinner, Sarah continued to be enthusiastic, and it emerged that Rolf, who had been a bit unsure of his brother-in-law's reaction, apparently, since upsetting the apple cart so thoroughly, would be coming back tomorrow. And tnat he and Sarah would stay on at Katerina until the end of this season's muster.

Lydia glanced at Joe. He'd obviously assured Sarah that Rolf would be welcome, which was only the sensible thing to do, but she couldn't help wondering what his inner feelings on the subject were, and closed her eyes briefly. Because, of course, she herself wasn't too good at reading his inner feelings, let alone sorting out her own.

He came to seek her out in her bedroom after Sarah had gone to bed.

She was standing in front of the door to the verandah, staring out into the night with her arms folded. She hadn't changed out of her khaki pants and dark green pullover. She didn't turn at his light knock and he didn't wait to be invited in. There was no reason that he should, she reflected. He had seen everything there was to see about her.

At the same time, when he put his arms around her from behind, she couldn't stop herself from leaning back against him with a sigh, and blinking a couple of ridiculous tears from her lashes.

'I think I can guess how you feel,' he said quietly.

'Can you?'

'As if everything that should be essentially private between us has been laid out and trampled on from here to Darwin.'

'You're so right,' she murmured. 'I even wondered whether they'd been laying bets. Talking of which, you won *your* bet hands down, Joe.'

'I'm not rejoicing. I wish I'd never made it. Lydia, can I look at you?'

He let her go and she turned slowly. And something inside her ached at what she saw. A man too good with women for his own good, perhaps. She winced inwardly to think that on first impressions she'd wondered what Daisy had seen in him—not that it had lasted long. Only moments, perhaps, before the impact of Joe Jordan had started to make itself felt.

The impact that now saw her standing in an unremarkable bedroom with twin beds, horribly pink chenille covers and furniture that didn't match, knowing he could make love to her anywhere and it would be heaven. Knowing that she loved everything about him. From his brown hair, that sometimes stood up, to his freckles, his sense of humour, his body, his hands, even the darkness of his moods, at times. But also knowing she hadn't made the same impact...

'If there are doubts,' he said gently, 'it's because I'm not the easiest person to live with at the best of times. Which is not to say we mightn't make it. But I think there needs to be a longer run-up. I think you need to see the really...the times when I know I'm being impossible but I just can't seem to help myself. The times when I'm going to curse Katerina for the hold it has on me and long for Balmain. When I get desperately sick of cows and yearn for bright lights and clever conversation, even though I know they won't hold me either.'

Her lips parted but he went on. 'I guess it's like a crisis, or a crossroad. I don't know how I'm going to react to it. I—'

'You could always find a manager. You could spend the wet season down south...' She stopped abruptly.

'Perhaps,' he agreed. 'But that's an example of the kind of decision I'm going to have to make. Give up journalism completely or try some other form of it, some part-time form of it? Try my hand at politics?' He shook his head. 'The only thing I know at the moment is, it's not going to be easy.'

'So, what do you propose we do?' she heard herself asking from what sounded like far away.

He took her hand. 'Come and live with me until you can really say whether you love me or hate me.'

'That sounds so sensible, Joe,' she whispered, 'but—'

'I know. It's also asking you to give up your job and your life down south. It's asking a hell of a lot, in fact, but I wouldn't even think of it if I didn't know you loved Katerina.'

'I wasn't going to say that.' She looked away and bit her lip.

He ran his fingers down her cheek. 'Tell me.'

'Well, the other side of me finding out if I could live with you is *you* finding out whether you are locked to me mentally and physically or—still standing on the outside.'

'I am—locked to you both mentally and physically—'

'No, Joe. If you were you wouldn't be proposing this. This very sensible, sane solution—I'm sure a lot of people would no doubt agree it is. But I don't see it that way. And, because of that, when Pete goes to pick up Rolf tomorrow I'm going with him.'

'Lydia—'

But she managed to smile at him through her tears. 'Joe, there's only one thing you failed to understand about me. You read me right in so many ways, you let me think I was dictating terms and going at my pace, and all of that got me over the final hurdle of laying Brad's memory to rest. But there's one thing you missed. The one thing you didn't see was that you led me all this way only to offer me second best. I can't accept it.'

'Would you seriously prefer a rush to the altar?'

'No. I'd seriously prefer you to know your own mind, but since you don't, and can only offer me something that's a sort of ''mostly marriage'' compromise but not the real thing, so we can cop out when the going gets a bit tough—'

'Lydia,' he said grimly.

'Since you can only do that,' she persisted, 'I'm going to say thank you for everything and please don't subject me to a Joe Jordan who's been thwarted. And just remember, when the right one does come along for you you'll know it, when where you live or what you do pales into insignificance beside not being *truly* together.'

'You don't think you're in control freak mode, do you, Lydia?' he said harshly.

She drew a breath. 'I'm not sure which one of us is a control freak, Joe, but it could just as easily be you. Goodnight.' She turned away decisively.

He went.

'So it finished just like that?' Daisy said two days later when she returned from the Musica Viva tour to find her younger sister back at home. 'He didn't try to stop you the next morning or—'

'No. Not that he'd have succeeded,' Lydia said. 'We were exceedingly polite. We'd had a bit of practice at that, which is just as well because Sarah was wildly curious. In fact Meg and I had a more emotional parting than Joe and I…and I don't regret it.'

'Say that again?'

This time they were in Daisy's bedroom as she unpacked.

Lydia shrugged after a moment. 'Of course I do.' She blinked a couple of times and sniffed. 'I feel as if I'll never be the same again, but…' She sighed and pleated her hanky. 'I wasn't the right one for him. It's as simple as that.'

Daisy glanced at her bent head and working fingers. 'I told you he could be moody and sarcastic. Perhaps you shouldn't take too much notice of it? I mean—'

'Daisy, this was different.'

'OK, but all the same—'

'No, tell me about you!' Lydia insisted.

Daisy sat down on the bed rather abruptly. 'I'm engaged.'

'*What?*'

'The oboe player,' Daisy said a bit dazedly. 'He—his name is Simon, by the way—he was waiting for me in Darwin when I got back from Katerina.'

'Daisy—'

'No, this is different, Lyd,' Daisy assured her. 'This really is different...'

Three months later Lydia had to acknowledge Daisy was right as she walked down the aisle behind her sister. Because it was hard to imagine two people more in love than her sister and Simon Hart, or more suited to each other, despite the age difference—which Daisy seemed to have long since disregarded, anyway.

After Daisy's wedding ceremony, at the reception in a chic restaurant, it was Chattie who took Lydia aside and looked her up and down in her beautiful champagne silk gown. 'How's it going?'

'Fine.' Lydia looked comically perplexed, as if this was a strange time and place to be asking that.

'I just wondered if this was a bit hard on you,' Chattie said.

Her aunt was looking supremely elegant in a navy suit, but she also looked determined and had a *you don't fool me for a moment* air about her.

Lydia sighed. 'Because it's made me think of my own wedding? Sure, but—'

'Because you're eating your heart out for a man who may not be perfection personified,' Chattie said baldly.

Lydia licked her lips. 'How do you know that?'

'You've lost weight—that dress has had to be taken in twice since the dressmaker started to make it—and I happen to know all about Joe Jordan.'

Lydia sighed. 'Daisy, I suppose.'

'Daisy,' Chattie agreed.

'This is still an odd time to choose. I'm sure Daisy spilt the beans a while ago.'

'She did.' Chattie paused and sipped her wine. 'But I thought, OK, let's see how you handle it. You obviously had your reasons for walking away from him. What I can see *now* is that you're not handling it very well—'

'This is still an odd time to choose,' Lydia insisted, with a spark of anger in her eyes.

'You aren't the easiest person to get through to, Lydia, so I thought I'd choose a time when you might be lacking some of your usual defences,' her aunt replied blandly.

To her horror, Lydia discovered she had tears in her eyes, because no one could know how difficult this wedding had been for her except her intuitive aunt.

'The thing is,' Chattie said gently, 'we're a lot alike, you and I. But I wouldn't like you to make the same mistake I made. Here, pet.' And she handed Lydia a lace-edged handkerchief from her pocket.

Lydia swallowed a couple of times and blew her nose. 'What was that?' she asked hoarsely.

'I turned my back on a man because I felt I loved him more than he loved me. It made me feel…vulnerable. It made me scared that I'd break my heart. I now know,' Chattie said slowly, 'that if I could have my time over again, even heartbreak would be preferable to this feeling I have to take to my grave that I should have given it a go.'

'Is...is it too late?' Lydia stammered, tears for her aunt now starting to well.

'Far too late. He's married to someone else with a teenage family.' She gestured.

'I think I need to sit down,' Lydia said.

When they'd found themselves a quiet spot in a couple of armchairs, Lydia said intensely, 'He manipulated me.'

Chattie raised an eyebrow. 'He must have known you well to be able to do that. How did he manipulate you?'

'He let me think I could manage him. He let me believe I made the decision to go to bed with him. That's the other thing. He knows *women* too well. There I was—' Lydia stopped, with a strangely futile expression in her eyes. 'Being superior about Daisy, and how she'd keeled over for him, only to find myself doing the same.'

They both glanced towards the bridal table, where Daisy and Simon were staring into each other's eyes and James Kelso was looking on indulgently. True to form, although he'd added a tweed jacket and a tie to his khaki shirt, James still wore jeans.

Then they looked at each other with identically wry smiles. And Chattie said, 'At least we don't have to worry about Daisy and what her biological clock may have got her into.'

'No. Thank goodness.'

'But he did ask you to live with him?' Chattie queried.

'Yes. For all sorts of good reasons, but not the best.'

'That may have been wiser than you think,' Chattie commented. 'Look, I'm not going to say much more, just this. The way it happened for you with Brad may have been the best and the easiest way. That doesn't mean to say it always happens that way. If you can't get this man out of your heart and mind, give it another go, my dear.'

'There's...what about...? My pride seems to be involved,' Lydia said unhappily. 'Not that I'm...' She stopped helplessly.

'I've always thought that a bit of pride is a good thing,' Chattie said. 'Too much is the opposite.'

A couple of days after the wedding Lydia was striding out along the walkway not far from home, across the cliffs that linked several beaches. It was overcast and showery, although not cold. There were storms out to sea and slanting pencil lines of rain on the horizon.

She'd been walking for a couple of hours and was on her way back when she sat down on a bench and pulled off her raincoat. Her hair was damp but she was hot, and there looked to be a break in the showers. She stared at the silvery patches of light on the dull pewter surface of the ocean, where thinner cloud was allowing the sun to admit to a slight presence on this otherwise grey and drizzly Sydney day.

Daisy and Simon were in Fiji on their honeymoon, her father was in Melbourne at a writers' conference, and her aunt was about to launch an exhibition of her work, so she was extremely preoccupied and had made no further comments on Lydia's love life. It was a weekday, but because she was on weekend duty at the vet practice Lydia had a couple of days off. Days that she was finding extremely hard to fill.

She'd tried to blame Chattie for this in her mind, but honesty had prevailed. Her whole life had been extremely difficult and hard to fill for the last three months. But of course Chattie *was* responsible for throwing down the gauntlet, so to speak. Responsible for making her face the growing conviction that she might have made an awful mistake. Why else would it be getting harder rather than easier to live without Joe? Why else were her thoughts always elsewhere? Precisely, up in the VRD of the Northern Territory.

Had the wet season commenced? she wondered. Had Rolf and Sarah moved out? Was Joe in residence at Katerina or Balmain? Had she been so self-engrossed she'd walked out on him when he'd really needed her? Had she accused him of manipulating her when in fact what he'd said was true? She could never have got over Brad any other way than to think *she* was shaping her life.

She sighed. One could be forgiven, she mused, for thinking he needed no one. But then, hadn't she been through a stage in her life when she'd thought she needed no one?

And how to give it another go, as Chattie had suggested? How to cope with rejection if Joe had decided he could live without her?

She closed her eyes as all these questions went round and round her mind. Then opened them as she heard a dog barking excitedly and saw two people walking towards her with a pale golden Labrador that looked just like Meg. Before she could blink the dog raced up to her and sat down in front of her to extend its paw lovingly.

'Meg?' she whispered. 'Is it you? No, it can't be.'

The couple, a middle-aged man and woman, had also stopped, and were smiling at the dog's antics.

'She's lovely,' Lydia said huskily. 'I knew another dog just like her; she also used to shake my hand. You've trained her well.'

'Oh, she's not ours,' the man said. 'She just appeared

out of the blue. She's got a note tied to her collar, addressed to someone called Lydia—would that be you? She seems to know you. She didn't offer to shake our hands.'

'Meg, it *is* you.' Lydia swallowed, and with shaking hands she untied the string attaching the note to the dog's collar and smoothed it open. It was a cartoon. A look-alike Joe Jordan on his bended knees. The caption said 'HAVE I BURNT MY BOATS?'

She looked around and he was there, standing tall and straight only a few feet away, as the middle-aged couple melted away. A different-looking Joe Jordan, in a grey suit with a white shirt and navy tie, although the jacket was hooked over his shoulder. But not only different because of that. A more serious, sombre person than she'd ever seen him.

'Joe?' she said dazedly. 'I… I…' She was shaking all over, she realised.

'Hello, Lydia,' he said, and walked towards her.

She started to get up, then stopped, and he stopped, and closed his eyes briefly. 'Don't run away from me, please.'

'I…' She swallowed, because some instinct had prompted her to flight. Some sense of self-preservation, perhaps, some fear that this couldn't be real.

'Can I sit down and talk to you?' he asked quietly.

'I…how did you find me, and…?' But she couldn't go on.

He sat down beside her and she thought there were new lines scored beside his mouth, and that he looked thinner. 'Your aunt told me where I'd find you. She also updated me with Daisy's news. You must be very happy for her.'

'I am. We all are—what else did Chattie tell you?'

He glanced at her. So far he'd made no move to touch her, and there was about six inches of clear space between them on the bench. Close enough, though, for Lydia to be acutely aware of him through all her senses. 'Nothing, other than that your father is in Melbourne. Should she have?'

Lydia breathed a little easier, although her pulses were still beating erratically. 'No.'

'How are you?' he said.

'Fine,' she lied. 'Uh—how are things up on the VRD?'

'Very wet.'

Lydia realised she was smoothing his cartoon almost frantically and willed herself to stop. 'This…is a bit of a surprise, Joe.'

'I know.' Once again he glanced at her, taking in the black vee-necked body suit she wore with jeans, her hair, her lips… 'Can I tell you about it?'

She could only nod.

'You asked me once whether I'd missed Daisy when she wasn't there. I told you no. But it wasn't the same with another girl. A tall, serious girl with a boyish stride, who shot from the hip—when she wasn't laughing and making me laugh. A girl who seemed to develop an almost mystical affinity with my home. A girl who strode the back roads of my mind even when I…tried everything to make myself forget.'

'Such as?' There was the faintest quiver to her lips that might, or might not have been a smile.

'Working myself to exhaustion. Fighting with myself over trivial things. That's all.'

'So you didn't try to forget this girl in the traditional manner?'

'No, Lydia. That would have been impossible, if you

mean finding myself another girl to take her place in my bed.'

'Joe...' Lydia paused and licked her lips. 'You may have been wiser than I realised at the time.'

'That was one of the disputes I had with myself.' He put his arm along the back of the bench behind her. 'Along the lines of who does this twenty-six-year-old girl think she is? A pillar of wisdom on these matters? And all because she happens to have been married once?'

Lydia moved abruptly, but his fingers rested lightly on the point of her shoulder and she stilled, because even through the black stretch knit of her top it was electric to feel his touch again.

'As with the other disputes I had with myself,' he continued, 'well, her point of view won hands down when I finally stopped and realised what I'd done.'

Lydia turned her head to look at him properly for the first time since he'd sat down beside her. 'Do you mean...' she asked huskily, but couldn't go on, and closed her eyes because she was still afraid to hope...

'I mean...' he said, and leant forward to kiss the tip of her nose, and then it seemed as if *he* couldn't go on.

'I mean,' he said at last, this time against the corner of her mouth, 'what we had was so special—where I lived, what I did, all those big decisions that I thought were going to be so difficult to make, they turned out to be nothing compared to the pain of thinking I might have lost you, and that, for good.'

'Joe...' Her lashes fluttered up and her eyes were wet. 'It's been three months.'

'I know,' he said bleakly. 'But I persisted in trying to sort some kind of a life out of the chaos, and I persisted in the belief that until I did I shouldn't drag you through the process, assuming I hadn't turned you off me completely.'

'So what changed your mind?'

'It was Meg, really.' Meg was now lying contentedly at their feet.

This time Lydia did smile. 'I know she's a charming and intelligent dog, but can she talk now?'

'No. Not in so many words. It was when I realised I'd alienated even her while I was tilting at imaginary windmills, so that she no longer sought me out or appeared to get any pleasure from my company...' He stopped and put both his arms around Lydia.

'This sounds absolutely bloody stupid,' he went on harshly, 'but perhaps it's a good idea to remember it, because that's what I can be like—that's when I realised what I'd done and that there was one simple key to my whole life, and it was you.'

'Thank heavens for Meg.'

He lifted his head and looked into her eyes. 'Do you really mean that, Lydia?'

She sighed a shuddering little sigh. 'Oh, yes.'

'So these three months haven't...?' He paused.

'They've been sheer hell,' she confessed, and put the palm of her left hand to his cheek.

He covered it with his hand, then took it away from his face and looked at it. It was the hand she always wore Brad's signet ring on, but it was bare.

'When?' he asked.

'When did I take it off? When I got home from Katerina. Because although I'd convinced myself,' she said, 'that I loved you more than you might ever love me, and although I thought I had succumbed like every other woman you'd known, I also knew I'd been released at last from the pain of losing Brad and was able to love another man.'

'You weren't like any other woman I'd known, Lydia. And you turned the tables on me completely. You let me love you then you left me because I didn't come up to scratch.'

'Joe—' she blinked at him '—I thought it was the other way around…'

'No, sweetheart,' he said definitely. 'I've been such a fool.' He released her hand and cupped her face. 'Because I can't begin to tell you how many ways I love you. I can't begin to tell you how arid not only my life has been but my soul has felt.' He paused and she saw him swallow, and realised he was speaking from the heart. 'But other things about me haven't changed. Such as the way I let you leave Katerina because I was convinced I was right when I was quite wrong.'

'I may have contributed.' Tears were slipping down her cheeks now and he smoothed them with his thumbs. 'I may have laid down the law occasionally myself. It wasn't easy for me to admit you were irresistible, Joe Jordan.'

He closed his eyes and leant his forehead against hers, and she felt the shudder of relief that went through him. Then he kissed her wet, salty lips gently. 'Will you marry me, Lydia? I still haven't worked out what I'm going to do, but at least half our lives will be spent on Katerina, if that's OK with you.'

'I don't think you need to worry about that. I love Katerina. As a matter of fact—and I started to tell you this once, then never did say it because I thought it may have been an indication that I'd gone overboard for you, and I had difficulty admitting that to myself, let alone you—'

'Ah. The night the ringer broke his leg?'

'Yes.' She laughed a little. 'It sounds ridiculous now, but I was going to say that I loved your Balmain house even to wanting one like it myself.'

'Not ridiculous at all. The list is building up,' he said with a wicked little glint in his eyes. 'You like my homes, you like my dog. Could you see your way clear to liking me enough to marry me?'

'Yes, thank you, Joe, I can.' And they laughed together until he started to kiss her...

It was Meg's growl that drew their attention from their passionate embrace to some walkers approaching.

'Perhaps we ought to go somewhere more private,' Joe suggested.

'What a good idea—how did you get here?'

'I flew myself from Katerina then drove from Balmain,' he replied. 'I didn't want to subject Meg to the indignity of a cargo hold, especially since I was sending her on such an important mission.'

'So you've never brought her down here before?'

'No.'

'Thank you,' Lydia said softly. 'But why are you looking so formal?' she asked as they rose and she pulled her raincoat on and he donned his jacket. It was starting to rain again.

'I had planned to approach your father and ask for your hand, having been threatened with him on at least two occasions.'

'Who—? You didn't tell me Daisy had also threatened you with Dad!'

'It must have slipped my mind,' he said wryly.

Lydia's lips curved. 'He's in Melbourne.'

'I now know that. It's not funny either,' he said gravely as Lydia gurgled with laughter.

'Yes, it is,' she insisted. 'My father is the worst dresser in the world. He never wears anything other than bush shirts, jeans and odd socks.'

'I see.' Joe Jordan stopped in the middle of the path. 'So I could have made a right fool of myself?'

'Not with me,' she disagreed. 'Somehow, the thought of you dressing in a suit to impress my father lends a whole lot of authenticity to this.'

'What about this?' he asked, hours later.

They'd driven to Balmain and gone to bed, where they still were after making love.

Lydia stirred and looped her hair behind her ears.

'I love the way you do that,' he murmured, 'but it's often a sign that something's bothering you.'

She pulled a pillow under her head and ran her fingers across his bare shoulders. She said nothing as she took in everything about him. The sandy-brown hair that often stood up in spikes. The faint hint of freckles, his hazel eyes—serious and with a question in them. And her emotions suddenly boiled over. The months of thinking she'd lost him and the cold ache inside her that that loss had produced claimed her. Tears welled, but she said simply, 'Nothing's bothering me—I was moved beyond words, that's all.'

'So it also had the stamp of authenticity?' he said into her hair, gathering her close. 'Don't cry—I could kill myself for being such a fool.'

'I'm not really crying. Well…' She paused. 'I felt like it so often, but never did—perhaps I need to get it out of my system.'

'Do you remember,' he said softly, 'taking issue with me over the way I eat my chips?'

'I…yes.' She started to smile. 'But what's this leading up to, Joe?'

'Two things—are you sure you really want to take on such an uncivilised idiot?'

'I…what's the other one?'

'Before we get on to that, I'm just trying to point out some of my deficiencies.' He stopped as she moved, then quietened in his arms.

'For example,' he went on gravely, 'how many men do you know who've taken you for an early-morning swim in a freezing, crocodile-infested pool?'

She dissolved into laughter.

He kissed her gently. 'That's what I was really trying to do, make you laugh. It's one of things I missed so dreadfully, not having you to laugh with.'

She sighed, but because of the sheer warmth that flooded her. 'Now,' she murmured, 'whilst your love-making left me feeling exalted, uplifted and wrecked—' her lips quivered '—*that* makes me believe you do love me, Joe. I don't know why, but it really does. How do you feel?' she asked.

He lifted the sheet aside and stared down at her body, then buried his head between her breasts for a long moment. 'Luckier than I deserve to be,' he said at last, with an effort. 'And not only that but locked physically and mentally to a lover who will very soon be a wife—and, for the first time in my life, no longer standing on the outside.'

'Oh, Joe.' She smiled at him gloriously and smoothed his hair down. 'Thank you for that.'

Lindsay Armstrong...
Helen Bianchin...
Emma Darcy...
Miranda Lee...

Some of our bestselling writers are Australians!

Look our for their novels about the Wonder from Down Under—where spirited women win the hearts of Australia's most eligible men.

THE AUSTRALIANS

Coming soon:

THE MARRIAGE RISK
by Emma Darcy
On sale February 2001, Harlequin Presents® #2157

And look out for:

MARRIAGE AT A PRICE
by Miranda Lee
On sale June 2001, Harlequin Presents® #2181

Available wherever Harlequin books are sold.

If you enjoyed what you just read,
then we've got an offer you can't resist!

Take 2 bestselling
love stories FREE!
Plus get a FREE surprise gift!

Clip this page and mail it to Harlequin Reader Service®

IN U.S.A.
3010 Walden Ave.
P.O. Box 1867
Buffalo, N.Y. 14240-1867

IN CANADA
P.O. Box 609
Fort Erie, Ontario
L2A 5X3

YES! Please send me 2 free Harlequin Presents® novels and my free surprise gift. Then send me 6 brand-new novels every month, which I will receive months before they're available in stores. In the U.S.A., bill me at the bargain price of $3.34 plus 25¢ delivery per book and applicable sales tax, if any*. In Canada, bill me at the bargain price of $3.74 plus 25¢ delivery per book and applicable taxes**. That's the complete price and a savings of at least 10% off the cover prices—what a great deal! I understand that accepting the 2 free books and gift places me under no obligation ever to buy any books. I can always return a shipment and cancel at any time. Even if I never buy another book from Harlequin, the 2 free books and gift are mine to keep forever. So why not take us up on our invitation. You'll be glad you did!

106 HEN C22Q
306 HEN C22R

Name	(PLEASE PRINT)	
Address	Apt.#	
City	State/Prov.	Zip/Postal Code

* Terms and prices subject to change without notice. Sales tax applicable in N.Y.
** Canadian residents will be charged applicable provincial taxes and GST.
All orders subject to approval. Offer limited to one per household.
® are registered trademarks of Harlequin Enterprises Limited.

PRES00   ©1998 Harlequin Enterprises Limited

Tyler Brides

It happened one weekend...

Quinn and Molly Spencer are delighted to accept three
bookings for their newly opened B&B, Breakfast Inn Bed,
located in America's favorite hometown, Tyler, Wisconsin.

But Gina Santori is anything but thrilled to discover her
best friend has tricked her into sharing a room with
the man who broke her heart eight years ago....

And Delia Mayhew can hardly believe that she's
gotten herself locked in the Breakfast Inn Bed
basement with the sexiest man in America.

Then there's Rebecca Salter. She's turned up at the
Inn in her wedding gown. Minus her groom.

*Come home to Tyler for three delightful novellas
by three of your favorite authors: Kristine Rolofson,
Heather MacAllister and Jacqueline Diamond.*

HARLEQUIN®
Makes any time special ™